Flames from the Earth

A Novel from the Łódź Ghetto

Translated from the Yiddish by Julian Levinson

Northwestern University Press ✦ Evanston, Illinois

Northwestern University Press
www.nupress.northwestern.edu

Printed in the United States of America

10 9 8 7 6 5 4 3 2 1

Library of Congress Cataloging-in-Publication Data

Names: Spiegel, Isaiah, 1906–1990, author. | Levinson, Julian, translator.
Title: Flames from the earth : a novel from the Łódź ghetto / Isaiah Spiegel ; translated from the Yiddish by Julian Levinson.
Other titles: Flamen fun der erd. English | Northwestern world classics.
Description: Evanston, Illinois : Northwestern University Press, 2023. | Series: Northwestern world classics
Identifiers: LCCN 2022041769 | ISBN 9780810145573 (paperback) | ISBN 9780810145580 (cloth) | ISBN 9780810145597 (ebook)
Subjects: LCSH: Holocaust, Jewish (1939–1945)—Fiction. | Jews—Poland—Łódź—History—20th century—Fiction. | Litzmannstadt-Getto (Łódź, Poland)—Fiction. | BISAC: FICTION / Jewish | LITERARY CRITICISM / European / Eastern (see also Russian & Former Soviet Union) | LCGFT: Novels. | Fiction.
Classification: LCC PJ5129.S6812 F513 2023 | DDC 839/.134—dc23/eng/20221104
LC record available at https://lccn.loc.gov/2022041769

To my parents, Sarah-Gitel and Moshe,

My sisters Clara, Miriam, and Iske,

Murdered in Chelmno, Auschwitz, and Shtuthof

1941–1944

Martyred

—I.S.

In memory of Maimon Obermayer (1916–1939)

—J.L.

CONTENTS

TRANSLATOR'S INTRODUCTION

> As a writer, I have never really left the ghetto. I still see the people, the faces, the suffering crowd . . . That whole period still lives inside of me like a dybbuk.
>
> —Isaiah Spiegel (1973)

Isaiah Spiegel (1906–1990) was one of the most beloved Yiddish writers to emerge from the Holocaust experience. He won nearly every major prize awarded to Yiddish writers, including the International Culture Congress Prize (1955), the Itsik Manger Prize for Yiddish Literature (1972), the Yankev Glatshteyn Prize (1977), and the Yiddish Writers Union Prize (1981). A two-volume collection of essays about his work was published to commemorate his eightieth birthday. His most devoted readers came from the global community we might call *Yiddishland,* with centers in Tel Aviv, Paris, New York, Johannesburg, Melbourne, and Buenos Aires. Nearly everyone in this dispersed world had been directly affected by the Nazi nightmare. Nearly all had restarted their lives in unfamiliar places after unimaginable losses, and for many, the Yiddish language itself had become their only true home. These readers turned to Spiegel's writing to revisit the traumatic scenes of the Hitler years in the company of a trustworthy guide, someone who survived more than four years in the Łódź Ghetto, Auschwitz, and a work camp in Saxony—and who managed to transform his experiences into compelling works of literature. His writings are infused with symbolism, ornate metaphors, subtle irony, and beauty. As one of his earliest reviewers put it, "Spiegel is perhaps the only one who has given us the precious gift of the true ghetto-tale, because he has solved the problem of organically combining the authenticity of facts with the power of a great tapestry."[1] Spiegel was embraced by his readers not so much because he told them things they did not know, but because there was something reassuring, even uplifting, in the way he shaped traumatic experiences into art.

As with most Yiddish writing after World War II, Spiegel's work has been marginalized on the map of Holocaust literature familiar to most English speakers. Although Yiddish was the primary language of the majority of those who perished in or survived the Holocaust, the number of works available in English translation hardly reflects the intensity and quality of post-Holocaust literary activity in Yiddish.[2] Yiddish writing about the Holocaust provides a precious record of the unique ways Jews steeped in East European cultural and religious traditions responded to the catastrophe. It also offers indispensable insight into life in the Nazi ghettos, where Yiddish-speaking Jews were by far the majority and where many, like Spiegel, endured the most abject conditions for as many as four years. In the English-speaking world, only a handful of Spiegel's stories are known. His most widely read work, "A Ghetto Dog" ("Niki" in Yiddish), had the benefit of being including in Irving Howe and Eliezer Greenberg's widely reprinted *A Treasury of Yiddish Stories* (1954) and in a series on National Public Radio in 1995, for which it was narrated by Lauren Bacall.[3]

But Spiegel's work deserves to be recovered not merely because it was written in Yiddish nor because he found devoted readers throughout the Yiddish diaspora. His works call for a wide readership today because the conditions under which he wrote, coupled with his rare sensitivity and insight, lend his work a unique authority and power.

At the time of Spiegel's birth, the city of Łódź had already developed from a small town into an industrial powerhouse to become Poland's second largest city. Spiegel grew up in a section of the city known as Bałuty (Balut in Yiddish), a neighborhood on the northern edge of the city, where more than half of its Jewish population of 170,000 lived (by World War II, the number would grow to 230,000).[4] A majority of Bałuty's Jews were steeped in traditional Judaism; most were Hasidic, though an influx of "Litvaks" from Lithuania, Belarus, and Ukraine in the late nineteenth century brought opponents of Hasidism into the city as well. While the city of Łódź was home to the most opulent Jewish bourgeoisie in Poland, nearly all of the Jews in Bałuty were exceedingly poor. Few of the ramshackle wooden houses in the area had electricity, sewage, gas, or waterlines. Spiegel's parents both worked as weavers in sweatshops connected to the city's booming textile industry.[5]

The eldest of eight children, Spiegel received a traditional Jewish education in a cheder and Talmud Torah. Nevertheless, the religious culture of his family reflected the modernizing ethos of Poland's urban Jews. His maternal grandparents had been Hasidim, followers of the Aleksander Rebbe, like most of the local Hasidim; but throughout Spiegel's childhood, his parents were moving away from strict orthodoxy. As he later put it to an interviewer, "My father was not an observant Jew [*keyn frumer yid*], he was a cultural Jew [*a folks-yid*]" (249). His father's outlook was epitomized by the fact that on Sabbath he would read aloud from a Yiddish translation of the great German Jewish historian Heinrich Graetz's multivolume *History of the Jews*. Spiegel gleaned from Graetz's sweeping history a model of Jewish peoplehood rooted in a collective memory punctuated by persecution and perseverance. These themes resonated powerfully with Spiegel's everyday experience on the streets of Bałuty, and they would later provide a larger context for the Jewish tragedy in World War II. At the same time, Spiegel's early exposure to synagogue rituals left a deep sediment of felt experience from which he later drew in his writing. He would continue to employ symbols and images from traditional Jewish practice, as in the image of his father's tefillin wandering lost down the highways in a poem entitled "1945" or the image in *Flames from the Earth* of a cadaver whose splayed toes recall the gestures made in the Priestly Blessing.

Isaiah Spiegel in 1955. Photograph from Yeshayahu Shpigl, *Vint un vortslen, noveln* [Wind and Roots: Stories] (New York: World Jewish Culture Congress, 1955), v.

Spiegel's early life was also shaped by wider Polish and German cultural currents. During the years of World War I, he attended a public school for Jews and Poles modeled on the curriculum of the occupying German forces. He later attended a Polish secondary school (The Royal Gymnasium of Engineer Rusak), where he studied Polish literature and wrote his first essays and literary experiments in Polish. He later recalled a period when he wore his hair long in emulation of a portrait of Adam Mickiewicz, the national poet of Poland. He also recalled trying to capture the image of a setting sun in a style derived from Mickiewicz's renowned epic, *Pan Tadeusz*.[6] Although the Jews of Bałuty were socially separated from the Poles, Spiegel also recalled that a few Polish families lived in his family's apartment building, and that one family had assisted him in carrying out a "secret beautiful affair" (259) with a Roman Catholic girl that lasted more than a year. These interactions with Poles and with Polish culture help to explain the deep current of romanticism that runs through his work as well as the complex, often sympathetic representations of Poles in his writing, epitomized in *Flames from the Earth* by the heroic Catholic bell ringer, Nikodem Załucki.

In the early 1920s, Spiegel completed a teacher-training program and found work in a Yiddish-language school in the Tsisho network (Central Jewish School Organization). The Tsisho schools were organized under the auspices of the Jewish Labor Bund, but despite the socialist ethos of the Bund, Spiegel himself was less committed to revolutionary politics than to the world of art. "I never belonged to any political party and still don't," he told an interviewer in 1973. "People naturally assumed I followed the Bundist line, but my only party is literature" (347). During this period, he began associating with literary circles surrounding prominent local figures Moyshe Broderzon (1890–1956) and Itzhak Katzenelson (1886–1944), who had helped to make Łódź a center for Yiddish cultural experimentation in the interwar years. The avant-garde literary and artistic movement known as Yung-yidish (Young Yiddish) had already begun to disperse by the time Spiegel arrived on the scene, but the Łódź literary community—and Katzenelson's house in particular—continued to offer a vibrant, supportive environment for aspiring writers.[7] Other writers in Spiegel's orbit included Miriam Ulinover, Yitskhak Berliner, Israel Rabon, Rikuda Potash, and

Yosef Okrutni—many of whom he would associate with throughout the years he spent in the ghetto (272).

Spiegel's first poems and stories soon began appearing in newspapers such as the *Lodzer Folkblat* in Łódź, the *Folktsaytung* in Warsaw, and the Communist-oriented *Frayhayt* in New York. In 1930, he published his first collection of poems, entitled *Mitn ponem tsu der zun* (Facing the Sun). The influence of European romanticism pervades these early works, as in the initial poem in the collection, where Spiegel announces in the first stanza the power of art simultaneously to construct and to reveal: "O, zet! Ikh boy a velt oyf vays farshvigene papir / Un shtey far aykh a yunger lets farshempt, farklemt" ("Behold! I build a world on this silent white sheet / I stand before you as a foolish clown, ashamed and choked with passion").[8] The poet's private life takes center stage in this early collection, even as his personal longings come to reflect a collective desire, shared by many of his contemporaries, to place Yiddish literature on the map of world culture.

Two important texts for Spiegel during his twenties were Oscar Wilde's novel *The Picture of Dorian Gray* and Lord Byron's play *Cain*, both of which he initially encountered in Polish translation. The appeal of *Cain* lay in the thrill of discovering a wildly heterodox, indeed a heroic, reading of a quintessential biblical antihero. Spiegel was so moved by Byron's reimagining of the figure of Cain that he resolved to translate the work into Yiddish. With the help of Alexander Harkavy's *Yiddish-English Dictionary*, a German translation, and David Frishman's Hebrew translation, Spiegel completed his Yiddish rendering of *Cain* in the late 1930s; the press of *Literarishe bleter* had even announced the imminent publication of it in the journal's August 1939 edition.[9] However, to Spiegel's lasting sorrow, the manuscript of the translation was lost during the German invasion in September. His Yiddish version of an English romantic text about a biblical character, read through Polish, German, and modern Hebrew translations, never saw the light of day. Nevertheless, the tale of its construction itself bears witness to Spiegel's polyglot literary influences during the 1930s, his lofty aspirations for Yiddish, and the ways the Nazi invasion interrupted this internationalist moment in Yiddish literary history.

A few months prior to the outbreak of the war, Spiegel married Rebeka Ungier, a graduate of Warsaw University (260). He found work as an assistant accountant, and the young couple settled in an apartment near the center of Łódź. In July 1939, their daughter, Ewa, was born. During this period, he was also hard at work on a collection of prose narratives about the lives of impoverished Jewish weavers in Bałuty. Like his *Cain* manuscript, these writings were lost during the Nazi invasion.

The occupation of Łódź began on September 8, 1939, a week after the Germans launched the Blitzkrieg assault that marked the official beginning of World War II. Nazi troops rolled into Łódź and almost immediately subdued the local population. Ethnic Germans (Volksdeutsche), who comprised roughly 10 percent of the city, welcomed the Nazis as their liberators; they cheered as the high command enacted policies with the aim of thoroughly Germanizing Łódź. By the end of the year, the city would be incorporated into the new German province of Warthegau, the city's name would be changed to Litzmannstadt (after a German hero from World War I), thousands of "repatriated" ethnic Germans would be moved in, and plans would be finalized to de-Judaize the city by forcing all Jews into a ghetto.[10] The push toward ghettoization was led by the German medical establishment, who relentlessly cast the Jews as a racial enemy and bearers of dangerous illnesses, from tuberculosis to lice to dysentery. Ghettoization was portrayed as a necessary "hygienic measure," a mass quarantine that would save the city from contagion and pave the way to a brave new *Judenrein* German future (Horwitz, *Ghettostadt*, 37).

Created in the northeast part of the city, the ghetto spanned parts of the Old Town and most of Bałuty, where the poorest Jews already lived. Soon it also included the semirural Marysin quarter, where the Jewish cemetery was located along with the train station and *Umschlagplatz* (collection point), where Jews would later be forced to assemble before deportation. To enable the continued use of busy thoroughfares by the non-Jewish population, the ghetto administration built three wooden footbridges connecting the Marysin section to the rest of the ghetto. The ghetto comprised 4.13 square kilometers (later reduced to 3.82), small enough for a horse-

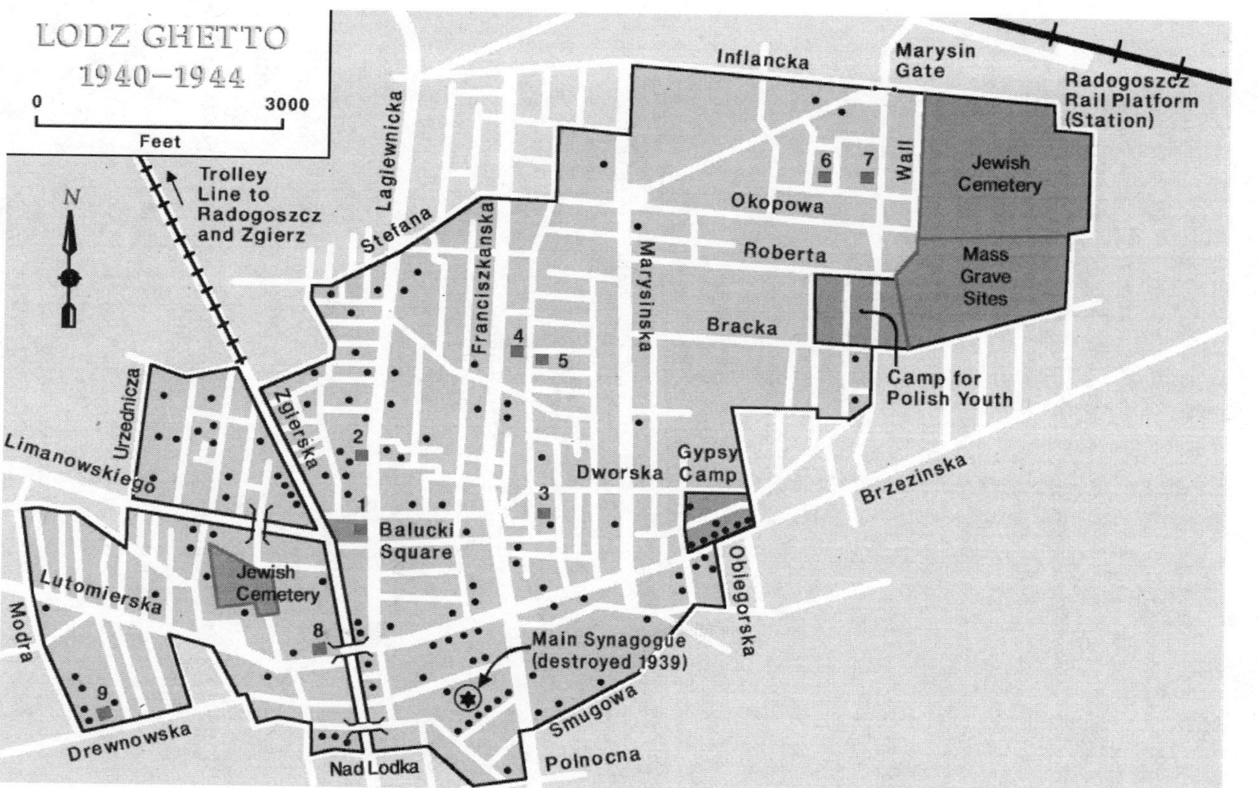

Map of the Łódź Ghetto, courtesy of the United States Holocaust Memorial Museum

drawn coach to circle its perimeter in under an hour. In February 1940, all Jews living outside the ghetto area were forced to abandon their homes and move into the ghetto, with a scant allotment of personal possessions. What the Germans called the *Übersiedlung* (the relocation) was described by one Jewish eyewitness as "a caravan of poverty."[11] To accelerate the movement of the Jews into the ghetto, the Nazi Order Police (the Orpo) launched an attack on March 6, 1940, known as "Bloody Thursday," in which 350 Jews were shot in their homes and on the streets. At the end of April, the ghetto was sealed. Barbed-wire fences were set up, guard posts installed, and any Jew caught escaping, or even loitering too long on the footbridges or elsewhere, would be shot. The Jewish presence in the city of Łódź had been erased from everywhere besides the ghetto, though the Nazi leadership had yet to determine their ultimate fate.

The Łódź Ghetto was one of the first ghettos to be established in Nazi-occupied Poland—and it was the last of the Polish ghettos to remain standing. It was the policy of the Nazi-appointed "Elder of the Jews," the controversial Mordechai Chaim Rumkowski, to make the ghetto as productive as possible.[12] He hoped to prove that Jewish labor was essential to the German war effort. "If he could just keep everything up and running, the clock might run out on the Germans, who finally would be gone, while the Jews would still be there, tending the machinery of production," the historian Gordon Horwitz writes. "This was Rumkowski's gambit. But it failed" (Horwitz, 315). In the ghetto, death from starvation and illness were daily occurrences. Within less than two years, Jews began to be deported from the ghetto and systematically murdered. A first wave of deportations to the killing center at Chelmno, located thirty miles northwest of Łódź, lasted from January to October 1942. At least five thousand Romani were also rounded up during the early years of the war and forced into the ghetto; every one of them perished. Finally, in the late summer of 1944, the ghetto was liquidated, and the remaining Jews were sent to Auschwitz-Birkenau. When the Soviet army entered Łódź on January 19, 1945, they found 877 Jews whom the Nazis had gathered as a cleanup crew. Their own graves had already been dug. Of the approximately 220,000 Jews who had lived at some point in the ghetto, about 5,000 to 7,000 managed to survive, mostly thanks to their sheer luck at having lived to see the liberation by the Allied armies of the killing centers at Auschwitz-Birkenau.

Spiegel was among those forced to move into the ghetto when it was first established. In the wake of the German's wave of violent evictions, Spiegel moved—together with his wife, their baby daughter, and his in-laws—into Spiegel's parents' crammed Bałuty apartment. Spiegel later described this period as a tragic sort of homecoming, whose brutality was tempered somewhat by his deep childhood connection to Bałuty: "I still knew every corner, every stone, every alleyway, every nook and cranny" (320). Spiegel's experience of "relocation" contrasted sharply with that of wealthier Jews of Łódź and, even more so, with the twenty thousand or so Czech and German Jews who were brought to the ghetto during the first months of 1941. Spiegel was acutely aware of the strained encounters between Jews from different social and cultural backgrounds. One of the stories he wrote soon after entering the ghetto, "The Family Lipshitz Goes into the Ghetto," insightfully describes an upper-middle-class family from Łódź that must acclimate themselves to their impoverished relatives in Bałuty.[13]

Spiegel gained employment thanks to his connection with the influential lawyer Henryk Naftalin, whom Spiegel later praised for his extraordinary support of the literary community (311). During the more than four years he lived in the ghetto, Spiegel held jobs at the Benefits Department, the Census Department, the Ration Cards Department, and the Finance Department. His tasks included assembling lists of the ghetto population for the Germans, tracking his fellow residents' health status and whereabouts, organizing health care for the infirm, and collecting housing fees. His work required him to roam throughout the ghetto and communicate with members of all sectors of the community. He also worked with the Archive Department, which was dedicated to documenting the history and daily lives of Jews in the ghetto (the fruits of their labors were later published as *The Chronicle of the Łódź Ghetto, 1941–1944*).[14] All of this work put him in touch with the life of the ghetto, but his closest contact came after work when he wandered about its streets and alleyways on his own. "Although I worked with people all day," he later explained, "it was only after my work that I witnessed the true face of the ghetto, the ghetto-man. This was, as it were, my true work" (356). These close visceral encounters gave him the material he would shape into stories.

But Spiegel was far from being merely an observer of the misery around him. Within a few months of his arrival, he personally experienced the ghetto in all of its brutality when his daughter died in front of him in the midst of a dysentery epidemic. She was a year and a half, and she expired, as he later put it, "of hunger, plain and simple." This devastating loss haunted him to the end of his life; it also fueled some of his most intense periods of writing. "When your world is destroyed," he said, "nothing remains besides intangible things—a word, a dream, the desire to shape your experience into a portrait" (316–17).

Following his daughter's death, Spiegel increasingly devoted his energies to writing. He joined an informal community of writers who gathered in secret at the apartment of poet Miriam Ulinover, his friend from before the war. Others in the group included Rivka Kwiatkowska, Chava Rosenfarb, Yoysef Zelkovitsh, Alter Shnur, and Rakhmiel Bryks. He also met from time to time with a group connected to Poale Zion, the Marxist-Zionist movement. They would meet covertly on the second floor of a building that housed a school. Short lyric poems were the predominant literary form produced by the writers who shared these literary evenings. "The writers in the Łódź Ghetto," Spiegel explained, "had short pencils, little time, and hardly any paper—and they were hungry. So they had to find the quickest way to say something about themselves, and that meant they turned to poetry" (339). For Spiegel and his fellow writers, these gatherings offered a chance to share intense emotions, as well as to continue conversations about aesthetic questions begun long before the war. Hunger was no longer the sole concern, Spiegel later told an interviewer, but "things that interested us as writers" (323).

One of Spiegel's poems from this period caused a stir—and not a little complication for Spiegel personally—when it was set to music and performed in public. Written soon after his daughter's death, "Makh tsu di eygelekh" (Close Your Little Eyes) evokes the form and rhetoric of a classic lullaby to make a grim commentary on ghetto life. As literary scholar Frieda Aaron has shown, the genre of the mock lullaby was widely used by songwriters and poets throughout the Nazi ghettos. In these highly self-conscious art songs, she writes, "the potentially soothing and sleep-inducing voice of the singer is capable only of abusive ironies and parodies of itself."[15] Spiegel wrote at least two poems in this vein; a second one is entitled "Nit keyn rozhinkes un nit keyn mandlen" (Neither Raisins nor Almonds). In "Close Your Little Eyes," he introduces a parent-singer addressing his child, but it turns out that the poem's speaker has no wisdom or comfort to offer. Both father and child share a common fate in a terrifying world:

> Close your precious little eyes,
> Birds are flying high,
> Circling around the skies,
> Above your tiny bed.
> A bundle ready in each hand,
> Our house has turned to fire and ash,
> Off we go, my darling child,
> To seek good fortune, where we may.
>
> God has closed the world so bright
> And everywhere is night,
> Darkness is awaiting us, with sorrow and with woe.
> We two are standing here,
> Trembling with fear.
> And where the path will lead, neither one can know.[16]

The poem took on a life of its own when Spiegel was asked by the composer David Beygelman to contribute a song for a concert to be held at the newly formed House of Culture. Transports of German, Austrian, and Czech Jews in early 1941 had added substantially to the already rich musical culture in the ghetto, and the House of Culture provided a four-hundred-seat venue for musical and theatrical events, complete with professional stage equipment and lighting. Beygelman arranged "Close Your Little Eyes" for an orchestra that included twelve violins; it was performed to a rapt audience on March 13, 1941. Seeing that a Nazi official was also present, Rumkowski became agitated when the audience erupted into applause. Fearing that Spiegel's ability to stir such powerful emotions would threaten the equilibrium he sought to create, he forbade the song from ever being played again.[17] In the ensuing days, Spiegel was fired from his job in the ghetto administration and narrowly escaped being deported.

Nevertheless, the song circulated throughout the ghetto, and it continued to be sung by Jews in the killing centers and, after the war, in displaced person camps throughout Europe. Spiegel's authorship was generally forgotten. "It became a folk song," he later said. Collected by Smerke Kaczerginski in his celebrated anthology *Lider fun di getos un lagern* (Songs of the Ghettos and Concentration Camps), it has joined the repertoire of Yiddish songs from the Holocaust.[18] Generally sung as a slow tango, its power derives from its poignant image of an anguished father trying in vain to soothe his child. Moreover, its haunting double meaning of "close your eyes" dramatizes the desperate effort of the victimized to regain a sense of agency: here the parent tells the child to close her eyes and fall asleep, as if to ward off her final sleep, that is, her death.

Poetry allowed Spiegel to vent his feelings of rage and despair, but the unprecedented horrors he witnessed every day in the ghetto seemed to call for a different mode of writing. In response to the grotesque reality he encountered all around him, Spiegel turned increasingly to prose narrative. "I couldn't fit life in the ghetto into the framework of a poem," he explained. "What I saw and experienced needed to be reflected in prose" (341). During his daily walks through the ghetto, Spiegel would note down striking scenes and events he observed, and in spare moments he would shape them into short narratives. He was particularly drawn to scenes of encounter between people: religious Jews quarreling about the meaning of their suffering, Polish and German Jews meeting for the first time, parents trying to revive moribund children, stout Nazi guards brutalizing emaciated Jews. Many of the stories that were later published focus on moments of agonizing decision: a woman who decides if she will chop up her fiancé's bed in order to warm her mother's apartment ("Light from the Abyss"); or a young couple who weighs the risks of attempting to escape the ghetto ("Snow").[19] Spiegel's goal in these stories was not to provide an exhaustive, objective account of ghetto life. He later distinguished his ghetto writings from the chronicles and diaries of figures like Emanuel Ringelblum and Oskar Rosenfeld. In contrast to their project, Spiegel used his poetic sensibility to infuse his narratives with symbolism, hoping to illuminate the deeper meanings underlying the scenes he observed, the intense loyalty that united Jews in the ghetto, and the idealism that enabled them to persevere.

In June of 1944, with the Nazis trying to stave off the Soviet approach from the east, Heinrich Himmler ordered the liquidation of the Łódź ghetto. Before the end of the summer, nearly all of the remaining seventy-five thousand Jews were taken either to Chelmno or Auschwitz-Birkenau. Spiegel was deported along with his wife and family in late August. Since the Nazi extermination campaign was shrouded in mystery given the isolation of the ghetto, Spiegel did not completely understand where he would be taken. Fearing the worst, he stashed most of his manuscripts in a cellar just before his deportation, bringing others with him in his luggage. On the railway platform at Auschwitz, his luggage was confiscated as he parted for the last time with his wife, his parents, and three of his sisters.

After three weeks in Auschwitz, Spiegel was taken along with four hundred prisoners to a labor camp in Siegmar-Schönau bei Chemnitz in Saxony. Calling himself a "correspondent" and announcing his skills with a typewriter, Spiegel was put in charge of organizing his fellow prisoners into work groups (his records later helped his fellow workers to procure restitution funds).

When the war ended, the labor camp in Saxony was shut down by the liberating armies and Spiegel found his way back to his native Łódź, which had been spared much of the destruction endured by other Polish cities. The Polish family who had taken up residence in the building where he left his manuscripts told him his writings had been thrown out a week earlier—but that the garbage cans had yet to be carted away. Sifting through mountains of debris piled in carts on the streets, Spiegel miraculously recovered some three hundred pages, many still legible (see next page).[20] He later described these recovered writings as his *sheymes*, using the term for the rabbinic charge to preserve pieces of paper inscribed with one of the seven

א בלעטל פונעם כתב־יד „די משפחה ליפשיץ גייט אין געטאָ“, אויסגעגראָבן
אין לאָדזשער געטאָ

A page from one of the manuscripts that Spiegel hid in the Łódź Ghetto and recovered after the war, "The Family Lipshitz Goes into the Ghetto." This page was printed in Yeshayahu Shpigl, *Vint un vortslen, noveln* [Wind and Roots: Stories] (New York: World Jewish Culture Congress, 1955), vii.

holy names of God. These recovered manuscripts became Spiegel's personal archive, as well as the material out of which he created his postwar literary oeuvre. They accrued an almost talismanic quality for him; he looked to them as a link between the ghetto and the postwar world, as well as a confirmation of one of the recurrent motifs in his writing: the movement from darkness to light.

In the years following the war, Łódź also became a thriving cultural center for refugees from the Soviet Union and survivors from elsewhere in Eastern Europe.[21] Spiegel got a job teaching at the reestablished Yiddish-language I. L. Peretz School and worked as the secretary of the Association of Jewish Writers and Artists, where he joined other surviving Jewish authors and artists in the work of mourning, commemoration, and cultural rebuilding. Among the celebrated figures who lived and worked in Łódź between 1945 and 1950 were journalist Leon Leneman, composer Shaul Berezovski, filmmaker Natan Gross, and writers Avrom Sutzkever, Rachel Korn, Chaim Grade, Smerke Kaczerginski, Binem Heller, and Isaac Janasovicz. There were also regular performances by renowned stage actors such as Shimen Dzigan, Yisroel Schumacher, and Ida Kaminska. Eight new Yiddish plays were produced between August and December of 1946 alone; in a single year, twenty-eight thousand tickets to the Yiddish theater were sold.[22] Spiegel too was an active participant in this lively cultural context in postwar Łódź. Indeed, when considering his postwar work, it is crucial to recall that he was far from being a lonely survivor reflecting on his losses in a vacuum. Instead, he saw himself as part of a cultural renaissance. "The most beautiful and creative community in Jewish history was destroyed, with all of its cultural treasures," he wrote in 1949. "But after the destruction, we witnessed the greatest wonder: the spiritual and bodily rebirth of surviving Jews after the catastrophe."[23]

In 1947, when the new Jewish daily newspaper entitled *Dos naye lebn* (The New Life) formed a publishing house of the same name, its inaugural publication was Spiegel's *Malkhes geto* (Ghetto Kingdom), a collection of eleven stories. Some of the stories were edited versions of the recovered manuscripts; others were based on stories Spiegel had lost but re-created from memory. A brief introductory statement on the first collection celebrates the work as "the first prose-book from restored Poland."[24] Indeed Spiegel's collection contains some of the first published literary narratives about the Holocaust. The cover art by Henryk Hechtkopf, a survivor of forced labor camps in the Soviet Union, reflects Spiegel's portrayal of the ghetto as a nightmarish realm of misery, dimly comprehensible to outsiders (see next page). But the lone human form dwarfed by menacing structures in Hechtkopf's image contrasts somewhat with Spiegel's deep mining of his characters' subjectivity and his recurrent theme of mutual dependence and loyalty.

A year later, in 1948, a second group of ghetto stories appeared in Paris under the title of *Shtern ibern geto* (Star Over the Ghetto); and the very next year saw yet another collection, *Mentshn in tehom* (People in the Abyss), which appeared in Buenos Aires. A pair of stories also appeared in *Di goldene keyt,* the recently formed Yiddish literary journal edited by Avrom Sutzkever in Israel. Meanwhile, Spiegel's poetry was published in Yiddish newspapers from Warsaw to Paris to Israel. Hence, within a half decade of the end of the war, Spiegel's writings began to circulate in the global postwar Yiddish literary community, while also helping to lay the foundation for what is known today as Holocaust literature. Spiegel's increasing awareness of the historical significance of his work—specifically the writings he had done inside the ghetto—is reflected in his decision to include dates for all of his stories. Even when he submitted his manuscripts to thorough editorial revisions or when he rewrote a story that had been lost, he was careful to identify the stories that he first wrote in the immediacy of the ghetto.[25] By this means, he ensured that the stories would carry the authority of an eyewitness account.

In 1951, after a two-year stint in Warsaw working as secretary of the Yiddish Writers' Union in Poland and an editor for *Yidishe shriftn* (Yiddish Writings), Spiegel emigrated to Israel. This was the period of the consolidation of Soviet rule in Poland, and many thousands of dissenters were being imprisoned; most of Spiegel's fellow Yiddish writers had already left. Together with his second wife—Charlotte (née Titel), a secondary school teacher from Lemberg with a master's in philosophy—Spiegel settled in Givatayim, just to the east of Tel Aviv. They would stay there the remainder of

The cover of *Malkhes geto*, Spiegel's first collection of short stories, with artwork by Henryk Hechtkopf. *Malkhes geto* [Kingdom of the Ghetto] (Łódź: Dos naye lebn), 1947.

his life. Spiegel worked for the Finance Ministry until 1964, when he was granted early retirement due to health problems. He recalled his first decade in Israel (the period when he wrote *Flames from the Earth*) as a time of great personal struggle. "I lived a lonely life," he said. "I was cut off from any sort of cultural milieu, and this added to my torment" (245). To be sure, there was a thriving Yiddish literary scene in Israel; but it was marginal to the concerns of most Israelis, who embraced a monolingual Hebrew culture and associated Yiddish with homelessness and victimhood.[26] Gradually, as the cultural status of the language rose throughout the 1960s thanks to the efforts of his friend Avrom Sutzkever and others, Spiegel received acknowledgment in the broader Israeli society as one of the most salient voices in Jewish letters, a status he had already enjoyed for many decades among his Yiddish readers around the world. His first collection of stories about the ghetto was translated into Hebrew, and selections were included in teaching materials for Israeli secondary schools.

He later explained that the idea to write *Flames from the Earth* came from an enthusiastic reader of his 1955 collection, *Vint un vortslen* (Wind and Roots). Writing in the New York–based *Di tsukunft*, the critic Alexander Mukdoni observed that the fifteen stories in Spiegel's *Wind and Roots* seemed to tell a coherent story, whose impact would be strengthened if their interconnections were uncovered. "Spiegel was born to write an important novel," he prophesied. "When we read the fragmentary stories in this book, we feel they are parts of a single work, a great tragedy" (350). Mukdoni, who was primarily a theater critic, understood that the tragic effect required a gradual unfolding—a sustained exploration of character, a building of suspense, and the revelation of the implications of decisions. And for this, a long-form work was required. Spiegel took the suggestion to heart, and eleven years later, he completed *Flames from the Earth*, which would be his one and only novel about his four years in the ghetto. To compose his work, Spiegel wove together as-yet unpublished wartime manuscripts with material he composed later. It was immediately translated into Hebrew and soon into French as well. The Hebrew version, given a new, more heroic-sounding title, *Arumim be-ṭerem shaḥar* (The Naked before

Dawn), was awarded the Levi-Garfinkel Prize for cultural achievement and hailed in the Israeli press as a triumphant homage to the martyrdom of millions. Hebrew University professor Dov Sadan called the novel a "precious gift" and a revelation into "the most difficult test that any Jew or human being has had to face, while hinting at the tipping point."[27]

As with his short stories and poems, Spiegel's *Flames from the Earth* fits into a larger constellation of Yiddish writings from and about the Łódź Ghetto, including the novels of Chava Rosenfarb, the stories of Rachmil Bryks and Leib Rochman, the poetry of Simkhe Bunem Shavevitsh, and the journalism and ethnographic writings of Josef Zelkowicz.[28] Using a variety of genres, these writers—the first three of whom survived, the latter two of whom did not—offer multiple views of the desperate struggle for existence that was daily life in the ghetto. For his part, Spiegel offers in *Flames from the Earth* an intense, emotionally charged narrative centered in and around the nightmarish world of the ghetto. Written in an evocative, lyrical prose style, the work reveals how daring acts of heroism were undertaken and unbreakable human connections were forged amid unthinkable conditions of violence and privation.

Notes

1. From the jubilee volume, *Yeshayahu Shpigl: In likhṭ fun der kṿaliḳer pen* [Isaiah Spiegel: In Light of the Flowing Pen] (Tel Aviv: Israel Book, 1986), 43.

2. For a discussion of the marginalization of Yiddish from the canon of Holocaust literature, see esp. David Roskies and Naomi Diamant, *Holocaust Literature: A History and Guide* (Waltham, MA: Brandeis University Press, 2012); and Jan Schwarz, *Survivors and Exiles: Yiddish Culture after the Holocaust* (Detroit: Wayne State University Press, 2015).

3. Irving Howe and Eliezer Greenberg, eds. *A Treasury of Yiddish Stories* (New York: Viking Press, 1954).

4. Robert Moses Shapiro, "Łódź," *YIVO Encyclopedia of Jews in Eastern Europe* (2010): https://yivoencyclopedia.org/article.aspx/Łodz.

5. There is very little information about Spiegel available in English. I have drawn most of my biographical account from a series of interviews

performed by Yechiel Szeintuch and Vera Solomon and transcribed in Yechiel Szeintuch et al., *Yeshayahu Shpigel—Prozah sipurit mi-Geto Łódź* [Isaiah Spiegel—Prose Narratives from the Łódź Ghetto], Hotsa'at sefarim 'a. sh. Y.L. Magnes, ha-Universiṭah ha-'Ivrit, 1995 (hereafter cited in parentheses). Parts of these interviews have been digitized: https://www.nli.org.il/he/audio/NNL_ALEPH004415800/NLI. These interviews are an indispensable resource for further research on the life and work of Isaiah Spiegel. Other sources I have consulted are Robert Moses Shapiro, et al., *Encyclopedia of the Ghetto: The Unfinished Project of the Łódź Ghetto Archivists*, Adam Sitarek, et al., eds., Archiwum Państwowe w Łodzi: Księży Młyn Dom Wydawniczy, 2017; David Hirsch, introduction to *Ghetto Kingdom: Tales of the Łódź Ghetto* by Isaiah Spiegel, trans. David H. Hirsch and Roslyn Hirsch (Evanston, IL: Northwestern University Press, 1998); Noah Gris, *Fun fintsternish tsu likht: Yeshayahu Shpigl un zayn verk, Eseyen.* [From Darkness to Light: Isaiah Spiegel and His Work: Essays] (Tel Aviv: Farlag Yisroel-bukh, 1974); and the introductions to *Mentshn in thom, geto-noveln* [People in the Abyss: Ghetto Stories] (Buenos Aires: IKUF, 1949) and *Un gevorn iz likht, lider* [And There Was Light: Poetry] (Warsaw-Łódź, Poland: Yidish-bukh, 1949).

6. For an outstanding recent translation, see Adam Mickiewicz, *Pan Tadeusz: The Last Foray in Lithuania*, trans. Bill Johnson (New York: Archipelago, 2018).

7. See Giles Rozier, "Yung-yidish," *YIVO Encyclopedia of the Jews in Eastern Europe* (2010): https://yivoencyclopedia.org/article.aspx/Yung-yidish.

8. Isaiah Spiegel, *Mitn ponem tsu der zun, lider* [With My Face to the Sun: Poetry] (Łódź, Poland: Alfa, 1930), 11.

9. For a discussion of Frishman's Hebrew version of *Cain*, see Mirjam Thulin, ed., *Transformative Translations in Jewish History and Culture* (Potsdam, Germany: Universitätsverlag Potsdam, 2019).

10. For background on the Łódź Ghetto, see Isaiah Trunk, *Łódź Ghetto: A History*, trans. Robert Moses Shapiro and Israel Gutman (Bloomington: Indiana University Press, published in association with the United States Holocaust Museum, 2006); Alan Adelson and Robert Lapides, *Lodz Ghetto: Inside a Community under Siege* (New York: Viking, 1989); Gordon Horwitz, *Ghettostadt: Łódź and the Making of a Nazi City* (Cambridge, MA: The Belknap Press of Harvard University Press, 2008); and Daniel B. Schwartz, *Ghetto: The History of a Word* (Cambridge, MA: Harvard University Press, 2019). For first-person accounts, see Oskar Rosenfeld, *In the Beginning Was the Ghetto: Notebooks from Łódź*, trans. Hanno Loewy and Brigitte Goldstein (Evanston, IL: Northwestern University Press, 2002);

and Lucjan Dobroszycki, *The Chronicle of the Łódź Ghetto, 1941–1944* [abridged ed.] (New Haven, CT: Yale University Press, 1984). See also Henryk Ross, *Memory Unearthed: The Łódź Ghetto Photographs of Henryk Ross*, ed. Maia-Mari Sutnik (Art Gallery of Ontario, 2015). Horwitz is hereafter cited parenthetically in the text.

11. Quoted in Julie Spergel, "Negotiating Diversity and Diaspora: Planting Chava Rosenfarb's Tree of Life in a Canadian Context," *Travelling Concepts* (VS Verlag für Sozialwissenschaften, 2010), 139.

12. For a fictional portrayal of Rumkovski, see Leslie Epstein, *King of the Jews* (New York: Coward, McCann & Geoghegan, 1979).

13. Isaiah Spiegel, *Malkhes geto, noveln* [Kingdom of the Ghetto: Stories] (Łódź, Poland: Dos naye lebn, 1947).

14. Lucjan Dobroszycki, *The Chronicle of the Łódź Ghetto, 1941–1944*, trans. Robert Lourie, et al. [abridged ed.] (New Haven, CT: Yale University Press, 1984). See also Robert Moses Shapiro, et al., *Encyclopedia of the Ghetto: The Unfinished Project of the Łódź Ghetto Archivists*, eds. Adam Sitarek, et al. (Archiwum Państwowe w Łodzi: Księży Młyn Dom Wydawniczy, 2017).

15. Frieda W. Aaron, *Bearing the Unbearable: Yiddish and Polish Poetry in the Ghettos and Concentration Camps* (Albany: State University of New York Press, 1990), 120.

16. Published under the title "Geto vig-lid" [Ghetto Lullaby] in Isaiah Spiegel, *Un gevorn iz likht, lider* [And There Was Light: Poetry] (Warsaw-Łódź, Poland: Yidish-bukh, 1949), 126. Translation mine.

17. See Trunk, *Łódź Ghetto*, 338.

18. Shmerke Kaczerginski, *Songs of the Ghettos and Concentration Camps* (New York: CYCO Press, 1948), 92.

19. See Isaiah Spiegel, *Ghetto Kingdom: Tales of the Łódź Ghetto*, trans. David H. Hirsch and Roslyn Hirsch (Evanston, IL: Northwestern University Press, 1998).

20. The story of Spiegel's recovery of his manuscripts was first published in the introduction to his first collection of stories (*Malkhes geto*); since then, it has become interwoven with the reception of his work, functioning as a "tale of origin" for Spiegel's postwar writing. Spiegel himself recognized the symbolic force of the story, using it to signify the rebirth of Yiddish literature in the wake of destruction. A more famous, but analogous, instance of recovered manuscripts concerns the archive of the Oyneg Shabes group in the Warsaw Ghetto. See Samuel D. Kassow, *Who Will Write Our History?: Emanuel Ringelblum, the Warsaw Ghetto, and the Oyneg Shabes Archive* (Bloomington: Indiana University Press, 2018).

21. Shimon Redlich, *Life in Transit: Jews in Postwar Łódź, 1945–1950* (Boston: Academic Studies Press, 2011), 68. See also Schwarz, *Survivors and Exiles*, 45.

22. Redlich, 72.

23. Isaiah Spiegel, *Un gevorn iz likht, lider* [And There Was Light: Poetry] (Warsaw-Łódź, Poland: Yidish-bukh, 1949), 3.

24. Isaiah Spiegel, *Malkhes geto, noveln* [Kingdom of the Ghetto: Stories] (Łódź, Poland: Dos naye lebn, 1947), 3.

25. Szeintuch et al., 549.

26. The role of Yiddish in Israel has been reexamined in recent years, revealing a much more vital cultural scene than previously assumed. See Rachel Rojanski, *Yiddish In Israel: A History* (Bloomington: Indiana University Press, 2020); Gali Drucker Bar-Am "'Our Shtetl, Tel Aviv, Must and Will Become the Metropolis of Yiddish': Tel Aviv—A Center of Yiddish Culture?" *AJS Review* 41 (April 2017): 111–32; Shachar Pinsker, "'That Yiddish Has Spoken to Me': Yiddish in Israeli Literature," *Poetics Today* 35, no. 3 (Duke University Press, 2014): 325–56.

27. Dov Sadan, back cover, *Arumin be-terem shachar* [Naked Before Dawn], 'Ivrit A. D. Shafir. Merḥavyah: Sifriyat po'alim, 1968. [Hebrew translation of *Flamen fun der erd*].

28. See Chava Rosenfarb, *The Tree of Life: A Trilogy of Life in the Łódź Ghetto* (Madison: University of Wisconsin Press, 1985); Rachmil Bryks, *May God Avenge Their Blood: A Holocaust Memoir Triptych*, trans. Yermiyahu Ahron Taub, afterword by Bella Bryks-Klein (Washington, DC: Lexington Books, 2020); Peretz Opoczynski and Josef Zelkowicz, edited by Samuel D. Kassow and coedited and translated by David Suchoff, *In Those Nightmarish Days: The Ghetto Reportage of Peretz Opoczynski and Josef Zelkowicz* (New Haven, CT: Yale University Press, 2015). See also David G. Roskies, "Yiddish Writing in the Nazi Ghettos and the Art of the Incommensurate," *Modern Language Studies* 16, no. 1 (1986): 29–36; and David G. Roskies, "Bialik in the Ghettos," *Prooftexts* 25, no. 1 (2005): 103–20.

Flames from the Earth

I

A Meeting in Snow

The fourth winter arrived all too early, swooping down over the shrunken expanse of the ghetto. A biting wind had picked up a few days earlier, blowing across the northern part of the city, over the crooked narrow streets of the Balut district, up through the dark distant fields of Radogoszcz, and around the vacant sandy lots near the Marysin train station in the east. Snow fell in glistening heaps on the rooftops and collected in the hollows and cracks in the walls. Window frames had long since been torn out of the houses, and the darkness inside the exposed rooms swallowed up the blizzard like spoonfuls of white medicine. Cold winds swept down from the heavens onto the snowy wasteland, spreading thin white sheets along the windowsills like delicate death shrouds.

Whenever a sharp gust blew through the empty courtyards, star-shaped snowflakes would gather on the ground in little mounds, sparkling like white pearls. Gust followed gust, their whistling becoming the voices of innumerable witches, howling and moaning as if at a ghostly wedding. Snow-filled clouds drifted overhead like strange, primordial creatures, their wings beating ceaselessly, drumming the snow down onto the earth below. Broken chimneys could be made out through the haze, standing on the rooftops like enchanted, petrified figures with severed heads, striking out with fierce arrogance against the armor of low-lying fog. Amid this empty white world, lifting the lid of a ghetto well would reveal crumbling stone and green mold spreading like death. With their chilly subterranean breath, the wells told tales of the old, vanished life. Secret streams of water still trickled somewhere deep below, refusing to be swallowed into the earth, just as milk continues to flow in a mother's breasts even after her baby has ceased crying. Water would spurt out of the crumbling wells when you least expected it. Maybe the wind had blown a sheet of ice off the opening; maybe an underground stream had surged upward, seeking a crack to escape the darkness. Some of the round, iron lids of the wells stood open, as if left by somebody seeking escape. Patches of bare earth near the base of the wells revealed blackened rags, scattered kitchen utensils, and the yellowing pages of holy books protruding like the partly exposed remains of corpses.

A transport had hauled the Jews away from this deathscape a year before. The few who remained kept to the other side of the bridge, creeping across at night to rummage in the dark through abandoned rooms and cellars, hoping to find an old potato, a few coffee grounds, a piece of bread lying in a corner. These nightly visitors would slink through forbidden places like hungry field mice digging for grain in a famine. Children would also cross over since they could fit more easily through the narrow cracks in the walls outside. They would tear open wooden floors, windowsills, wells. They would rummage through heaps of old trinkets left by those who had been deported. In this abandoned part of the ghetto, even the shadow of a Jew was forbidden. Rumors were going around about the Germans' imminent plans for the abandoned houses and courtyards.

Meanwhile the brutal Polish winds coated the land in snow, giving it the look of a long-abandoned cemetery. Then, in the middle of the month of Tevet, the storm winds died down. On the northern end of the city, the outlines of the forest could be made out through the smoky fog. Under the heavy sky, the snow all around was tinged with blue. As dawn broke, hunched shadows could be seen, creeping through the narrow streets and empty courtyards, their faces concealed. When these figures reached the bridge connecting sections of the ghetto, their footsteps would come to a sudden halt. Their feet, covered in dirty rags, seemed no longer willing to carry them. Black Jewish eyes would emerge from the shadows. Were these strange figures shades risen from a dim medieval past? Where did their destinies lead? What secrets did they conceal beneath their torn clothing? As they slipped quietly across the bridge, what fate had been ordained for these forsaken people?

✦

Day after day, Vigdor would cross the bridge, mingling with thousands of other Jews. Fewer and fewer remained after four years of ghetto life. As he peered at the faces around him, he was met with deathly cold stares, as if the last sparks of Jewish life were being snuffed out before his very eyes. He felt as if he, too, were being engulfed by the dark forces controlling his people's fate, but unlike so many others he had not fully surrendered to the hunger. He was like a tree cut off at the roots, and so he dug deeper into the earth's dark bosom to find what he needed to grow again.

Mysterious reserves of strength allowed him to maintain the appearance of a human being. Although the stream of blood flowing to his heart was thinning out, neither his feet nor his hands had lost their form. His face was jaundiced, but swollen bags had not appeared beneath his eyes. True, the muscles of his arms and shoulders had withered away, and his flesh, transparent as glass, was like loose dough that would never rise. Yet at times a rosy glow came over his face, returning color to his sunken cheeks.

Vigdor was ashamed of the strength in his appearance and movements. Many around him had swollen faces and feet. Oh, the beauty of something as simple as human feet! But could these still be called feet? The gazes of his fellow humans repelled him; in their eyes he saw only the fiery glare of animal rage. Stares of fierce suspicion seemed fixed on him for days on end. Surely he must have a hidden source of food they couldn't find. Surely he'd be one of the survivors. How else could Vigdor's father-in-law, a man well over sixty, walk without a cane? And why did Vigdor himself barely show signs of hunger? Was it because Vigdor's family on his mother's side came from a line of wealthy timber merchants, horse traders, and estate managers?

One way or another, he seemed buoyed up through the dark years of the ghetto by generations of strong Jews, their ancient roots, the sheer force of Jewish stubbornness. Walking among the throngs on the bridge, Vigdor did not look like a man who'd already spent years in the ghetto, who'd outlived his wife and five-year-old daughter, as well as so many others. On his way to work (oh, God, what work!), he would gaze from the bridge toward the southern end of the ghetto, where the streets led to the free part of town. He could just make out gray buildings through the fog, shimmering as if in a dream. The thought of free men filled him with painful longing, and his hands trembled. An image of home flooded into his mind, his old home on a distant side street in a part of town now forbidden to him. He envisioned his graying father-in-law pacing nervously in the dark rooms. The old man had refused to abandon his books, neither Goethe's *Faust*, nor the commentaries of Maimonides. From the first days of the Nazi occupation, his father-in-law had immersed himself in the German classics. A former yeshiva student from a poor family, he'd returned to his secret passion for books, reading several at a time, leaving a white card in each as a bookmark. When he'd been forced from his home, his only thought had been to bring along his favorites—Yiddish, Polish, German—and an oversized volume of the Psalms. He'd carried them into the ghetto in a bag over his shoulder.

Vigdor had never forgotten his father-in-law's words: "I don't need anything else. Only a few books—with a few books we'll survive the Germans."

Vigdor felt trapped in a dream in which he was taken from his own world and deposited on a different planet. He was sure everything would go back to how it had always been. Could it be that the world in all its vastness, the neighbors with whom Jews had shared the same ancient Polish soil—that everyone should suddenly shun them? How could the world be indifferent when an entire people was sent to suffocate in the ghetto?

Meanwhile, the seasons had passed. Springtime gave way to the wicked months of summer, when the lonely streets of Balut seemed to burn. The sun would hang in the vast blue sky like a huge, unmoving tear. Then the winds would sweep up from the sandy flats beyond the ghetto cemetery, howling like demons driving summer away. And now this winter, the fourth in the ghetto, was worse than all the previous ones. The winds slashed like the beaks of cruel birds, tearing the shingles off roofs. Many people thought they heard human voices in the winds. As evening fell, the voices seemed to grow nearer. But at night they were silent, and no moon shone. In the icy void of the sky, the stars seemed long dead.

✦

Dawn broke blue and cold as Vigdor crossed the bridge. His hands were buried in a threadbare overcoat, which the wind seemed intent on tearing away. The precious warmth of the chicory coffee he had just swallowed was lingering in his belly, along with its bitter taste. He didn't know why today he took more time than usual to gaze at the city below, which for years now had felt like a foreign land. Bathed in winter sun, it almost looked cheerful. The outlines of houses, stores, courtyards—all were clear in the early morning light. As Vigdor made his way down the stairs, he noticed mounds of newly fallen snow, which reminded him of piles of dirt alongside freshly dug graves. Turning toward the ghetto yard, he saw hundreds upon hundreds of feet marching onward; he saw hunched figures whose gaze never lifted from the snow on the ground. They had long ago lost the will to raise their heads.

Groups of people clustered at the tops of the frost-covered stairs. You had to grip the railing to avoid hurtling downward. Vigdor was pressed between crowds of people, dragged along by the current. At such moments, he felt he was rejoining the last scattered remnants of human life. A small sense of comfort came from the knowledge their fate was shared. His bitter gloom seemed to dissolve, and he felt a warm shimmering in his heart. But the crowd quickly dispersed into the wide main square of the ghetto, and, lashed by wind and snow, Vigdor was thrown back once again into his solitude.

Each time he crossed the bridge he was haunted by memories of the past four years. Images of the transports flashed before his eyes, countless Jews carrying bags and bedsheets and kitchen appliances, making their way across the bridge, heading who knew where. Their faces betrayed an eternal faith in human justice. Over the years, any remaining powers of resistance had left their bodies and their souls. Vigdor himself, a tiny speck alongside the great mass that had been moved out of the ghetto, felt that something inside had given out, as if a flame had been extinguished and only the wick remained. He did not belong to those whose blood burned constantly with the spirit of revolt, but when he pictured the fate of the Jews who had been taken away, his body convulsed with a jolt of rage. How had the Jews submitted to such humiliation? How had they permitted the Germans to hold them captive with thin wire? Why did they bow their heads, begging for a spoonful of gray, watery soup? Was it the unconquerable fear of death? Or was this simply how Jews had always behaved through the long centuries of bitter exile?

Crossing over the snow-covered bridge, Vigdor felt himself nearly dissolve into the masses of people. He was ashamed to find his eyes filling with tears. Overcome with hatred for himself and for his weakness, he clenched his fists, summoning the dignity to lift his head and look toward the city. There was the immense free world, refusing to share itself with the Jews. As he squeezed his fists tighter, he seemed to be pumping blood into his veins. He sought a friendly face in the crowd, someone to confide in. Maybe he could offer someone the message of hope he felt he had been entrusted with. Maybe he could comfort one of these dying faces.

As he descended the steps, he found himself following a short and slight figure for no apparent reason. Suddenly somebody seized him from behind in a warm hug. He turned around and wanted to cry out at once, but his voice caught in his throat: peering up at him was the tender face of a young woman. He stared into her eyes with wonder. The impatient throngs spat angry words as they pushed past the two figures facing one another in the snow.

"Gitele!"

He grasped her swollen hands.

"Vigdor, Vigdor!" she said, the sounds repeating in a chilled, quavering voice.

Only now did he see her face clearly. Dull green eyes peeked out from beneath a tangled shawl. Her eyebrows were interlaced with snow, her face damp, lashed by the icy wind. A ragged coat hugged her body, giving her a boyish look.

Vigdor cradled her hands, struck by the power of his affection for this girl who had come to him as if from a foreign world. She was beautiful, even in her oversized wooden clogs and with her face scarred from smallpox. No, even years in the ghetto could not stamp out the blooming face of youth. A feeling of shame seized him, seeing her sudden beauty in this hideous place. His heart beat faster. He lowered his head and waited. The silence that settled between them created a bond of unexpected intimacy.

"And Zelda—Zelda's here too?" he stammered.

She lifted her eyes wearily.

"Yes—she's sick."

"What does she have?"

"Tuberculosis. She hasn't got long."

Vigdor struggled for a breath in the icy wind, but the girl's words made his chest tighten.

"And your father?"

"Dead—last year."

"And your mother?"

"Deported."

She spoke in a whisper, her head slightly bowed, while the cold motionlessness of her features and her gray pallor momentarily reminded Vigdor of a plaster mask. Only the look in her eyes reassured him of her vitality. She spoke of the dead and sick as if they were abstract figures in a distant land. Vigdor was disturbed by the indifference in her voice. He released her cool hands, pained at the thought of how quickly the dead disappeared here, how soon their memory was erased.

She removed her scarf, brushing the snow from her hair. Now he sensed that she was holding back tears. Vigdor looked at her intently. Yes, they were tears, though suppressed ones, like those of a child who doesn't yet know the great relief weeping brings.

"Are you all alone, just the two of you?"

The girl again shielded her face with the scarf.

"Just us two. It'll be just me before long."

They moved on from the bridge with its endless stream of people. On this side of the ghetto, there were large empty lots and the scattered debris from ruined houses blocked the road. People scurried around broken boards and fences on their way to work. Wind swept up clouds of snow mixed with dust, casting sparkling crystals every which way. Vigdor felt energized, even excited, by Gitele's presence. A long-dormant feeling of desire stirred within him. Then he was troubled. This was *her* sister after all—Zelda's sister.

"Will you come visit us?" Her voice came to him as if through fog. "You did once before. Remember?"

He tore himself away from his fantasy; the icy breath of the wind returned. He held her trembling hands once again.

"You'll come?" she asked.

They walked on together down a narrow street, lined with dilapidated houses. Tufts of weeds and nettles, survivors of the summer, crept out of tiny cracks in the street, and small paths snaked between wire-enclosed flowerbeds, where Jews had grown vegetables in hopes of cheating their hunger. The abandoned beds were barely visible among the mounds of snow. Withered reddish leaves mingled with hardened clumps of soil.

"Come to us, Vigdor. Do it for her—this might be the last time you'll see her." Her voice was lost amid the gusts of wind blowing from the open field. Suddenly she tore herself away and ran off.

"Come, come and see us." Her last words were borne by the wind. He waved after her and bowed his head.

Left there standing alone, Vigdor felt the frozen solitude around him all the more acutely. He had been expelled from a warm bosom in the secret core of winter onto the desolate streets of the ghetto. Maybe it wasn't her he'd seen at all, but a mirage created by a whirlwind of snow. Dense fog hung in the frozen, leaden sky, as if determined to block the sun forevermore. A low moaning reverberated like a ghostly chorus through the empty field. Vigdor's eyes were drawn to patches of ruddy dirt peeking out from under the snow covering the makeshift vegetable gardens. He began to run. His only thought was that he needed to escape. But the more he tried to flee from one alley to another, from one courtyard to another, the more he felt arms reaching out for him as though a ghost had suddenly awakened beneath the sheet of snow. Now the gaps in the snow cover looked like countless eyes following him as he ran. He found himself among the broken shards of the ghetto wells, whose disfigured shapes seemed like the stony forms of the undead. The snow was deeper here, and Vigdor was sure he would sink deeper and deeper in, but the icy wind kept whipping it in swirls around his head, uncovering the earth, exposing red mud that looked like freshly drawn blood. The snow quickly piled up over the muddy earth once more, as if concealing evidence of a crime. Overcome by fatigue, he fell to the ground—like the colossal wing of a slaughtered bird.

2

At the Bedside of the Dying

Two gates—folded wings amid a low-lying tangle of barbed wire—stood on either side of a street between the northeast and western sections of the Jewish quarter. The gates were almost always locked. Only in the brief moments they opened could a Jew enter the free world outside, where an endless succession of blue trams passed by on their way out of town, with closed doors and cold, indifferent gentile faces pressed against the glass. Twice a day, at dawn and dusk, masses of Jews would gather before the gates, waiting for them to open. At the command of the German guards, the crowd would rush through the gates and cross the street in a disorderly throng of swollen legs and clattering pots and pans. On their way across, many would pause and gaze northward, where the road sloped down before climbing a steep hill and finally disappearing at the horizon. There, at the farthest point, tiny dark blue spots appeared: trees dotting the road. Trees. A forest. An otherworldly vista shimmering, not so very far after all.

While the Jews crossed the road, a German would sometimes stop someone at random and force him to turn around and show the yellow star on his coat. With hands protected by thick gloves and a face reddened by the cold, the German would keep his distance, avoiding the contamination of the Jew's breath. Meanwhile, the Jew would savor a momentary glimpse of the free road, expecting at any minute to feel the German's grip on his shoulder burning like the stab of a needle. Soon the ordeal would be over, and the Jew would rejoin the others, marching with outstretched arms, amid the metallic banging of pots and the infernal clatter of wooden clogs. It was a relief to reach the other side of the ghetto, to be surrounded once again only by Jews, by the familiar ashen faces—with the familiar look of dread in their swollen eyes.

To reach Zelda's street, Vigdor needed to join the crowd rushing between sections of the ghetto. As he entered the narrow strip that belonged to the free, unbounded world, he felt blood rushing to his temples. He was overcome again with shame at himself and his fellow Jews. It was as if a shadowy cloud had settled over him, darkening his vision. He couldn't understand what was happening. Why did the world refuse to help? How could everyone on the other side go on with their work? Why did their musicians go on playing their music? Why did they celebrate their holidays? Why? Why?

Hounded by these thoughts, Vigdor reached the other side of the ghetto. As he passed the rotting wooden houses, he was followed by innumerable staring eyes. In every Jewish face Vigdor saw the visage of his dead father. After only a short time in the ghetto, his father's features had taken on a strange, unfamiliar look. As the months wore on, his father had become nearly unrecognizable, as if his true face were concealed behind a mask, the face of hunger, swollen and flushed. At last, only the familiar look in his eyes remained. And now, the whole ghetto seemed to be watching Vigdor through his father's entreating eyes. Vigdor kept his head down as he walked the streets. He averted his gaze as if from a vision of horror. But still he felt pursued at every step by eyes peering out of every crevice in the walls, from every window and every staircase, these eyes that conjured up the final vision of his father begging mutely for help.

Vigdor had waited impatiently for night to fall. Now he was hurrying to see Zelda on her deathbed. Would he get to see her once more? Could he make it in time? He pictured her as she had been when they last met. Long black hair, pale skin. The whole business still puzzled him—a sudden, intense love affair that had ended almost as quickly as it began. And then came the great tragedy for the Jews; their sweet romance couldn't possibly survive the war. They were still young and inexperienced, and in the chaotic early months of the German occupation, each had gone separately into the ghetto with their families. There were so many things to worry about: hunger, deportation, the sudden death of so many people they loved, and the past was erased from their minds. Maybe it had simply been the dizzying pace of the ghetto, the perpetual comings and goings of Jewish families, throwing everything into confusion. But the truth was that in all these years of the ghetto their paths had crossed only once.

New shipments of Jews arrived constantly from nearby towns, replacing the frightened, silent men and women borne by innumerable convoys to unknown destinations. Death hovered like a bird of prey over the hills around the city, descending on people from places as far away as the banks of the Rhine, Maine, Donau, and Vltava. A new diaspora brought whole communities of foreign-looking Jews from Western Europe into dreary Polish cities, narrow ghetto streets where Eastern Jews swarmed as if it were the Middle Ages. Clutching their remaining possessions, the newcomers were greeted by centuries-old synagogues and walled-in areas built for those linked by flesh and blood to a shared Jewish fate. Some were convinced it was a sign of something miraculous. Maybe an evil hand had swept up Jews from every corner of the earth as a prelude to the day of redemption. Such a steep plunge into an abyss of evil could only be followed by an ascent into the light. After such long darkness, a new day would dawn, a field of flowers would blossom beneath a sky of eternal goodness, protecting everything on earth—human, beast, bird, and plant.

In the ghettos of the old Polish cities, the boughs of a huge tree were being regrafted onto an ancient stump. Its branches stretched over vast expanses, as far as the banks of mournful velvet-colored Polish rivers. The ghettos greeted these distant branches with the sad smile of a shamed mother visited by her estranged children.

Yet in this human mass, in the daily struggle against sickness and death, in this Jewish pandemonium, Vigdor himself was beginning to forget his former life. An animal vigilance over his constantly threatened existence kept him on guard day and night. From time to time a glimmer of light shone in him, as a spark bursts from coals in a fire, only to be extinguished in an instant.

✦

Twilight descended on the ghetto. As Vigdor walked past deteriorating houses, a furious gust sent clouds of snow across the sky, blocking out the light of the stars. At the end of an alleyway, just past the ghetto cemetery, he came to a courtyard filled with deep snow and scattered debris. There, at last, he found the staircase that led to a dark hallway.

He opened the door to the red glow of a lamp, winking like a demonic eye. The light was refracted through a halo of steam rising from a low stove. Gitele appeared from the shadows and guided him toward a group of men sitting around a table near a bed. They welcomed him with faint smiles; some extended bony hands. He recognized many from the streets of the ghetto, though he had never spoken with any of them. Their cheeks were hollow, their eyes bloodshot. Vigdor could hardly discern the familiar Jewish features, with only their thick black hair as assurance that he was among his own people. They didn't speak Yiddish, but a strange mixture of German and Czech, with scattered Hebrew phrases borrowed from old Jewish prayers. Gitele drifted away and Vigdor approached the bed. For a moment, he could see nothing in the dark but a sunken mattress and a chaos of rags. Then he heard a creaking sound among the old boards, and something stirred within the shapeless mass, a woman's hand reaching toward him.

"Vig . . . dor?"

He leaned over the bed to make out the feverish whisper rising up toward him. Her long fingers hovered in the air. As he took hold of them, he felt their clamminess and imagined she was already dead. Around the table, the strange men covered their faces with their hands and seemed to be holding their breath.

Vigdor was seized with fear—had he fallen in with an assembly of ghosts? The shadowy figures sitting bent over the table, the pale hand suspended before him, the roar of the night wind rising from the cemetery that filled the room with the calls of solitary night birds—all of it made him feel he had been abandoned in a remote land, among shades of people long dead.

He slumped down on the bed, squeezing Zelda's fingers. Gitele approached again and murmured: "Yes, Zelda. It's Vigdor. You recognize him, don't you? Vigdor has come to see you."

Her hand fell back onto the blanket, trembling like a butterfly. Vigdor leaned over and saw, in the dim light of the room, a small, terrified face. Her rapid breathing shook the blanket covering her body, and when she tried to sit up, she immediately collapsed back onto the bed, stammering with what seemed like her last breath: "The vi . . . violin . . . Anton . . ."

A pivotal moment from Zelda's life flickered in her memory, blotting out the present moment. Two years before, after she fell ill, a stranger had appeared at the door of the room she shared with Gitele. He was so emaciated that it pained Zelda to look at him. The stranger stood motionless before her for a long time, his head bowed in shame, trying to speak. He told her his name was Anton Kraft. Zelda beckoned him toward her bed, and he bowed several times as though begging her to forgive him. He seemed almost to float above the ground, and Zelda imagined he was a sorcerer, possessed by distant, evil spirits. A look of fear twisted his goyish features as he drew a small black bag from inside his jacket. It contained a few pieces of hard bread and a cluster of sugar cubes. In a stammering voice, he begged the girls not to refuse him a tiny favor. Every week, after rations were handed out, he would bring them a piece of bread and some sugar—not as a gift but in exchange for hiding his violin. Otherwise, he didn't know what he would do with it. He begged them not to refuse. Please. Every week. A piece of bread, some sugar. Just not to have to hand over his violin to the Germans.

The moment Zelda accepted the sugar, she was overcome with remorse. Maybe these few pieces of sugar were just enough to save this poor stranger. How much could he need to survive? As for her, she felt she had now crossed the final borderline. Her body was already beginning to devour her flesh and consume her last drops of blood.

3

The Dead Stradivarius

So Anton left his violin in the sisters' room for safekeeping. It was a precious instrument, an eighteenth-century Stradivarius that originally belonged to a concertmaster from Prague. Its varnish emitted an otherworldly glow, hidden now as it lay beneath the bed in the darkness of a padded case. The barely remembered lives of countless generations lay entombed within the violin. Its majestic fingerboard conjured up the beauty of a lost world, violet sunrises, iridescent sunsets over the Alps and the Sudetenland, the rustling waters of the Vltava River keeping shepherds and solitary travelers company as they strolled through the green valleys.

And now, as Vigdor looked on, a hunched shadow arose from the group of assembled men and approached the bed. It was the one Zelda had called Anton. He reached under the bed and gently lifted the black case. Then he turned slowly around and laid the violin on the table as if preparing a holy ceremony.

Zelda's sickroom had become a gathering place for Czech and German Jews from the courtyard, together with a few young people born and raised in the streets that now made up the ghetto. By some miracle, these young Jews from Balut had escaped deportation. During their first months in captivity, these former peddlers and porters had hidden away the iron handles of their abandoned carts, along with knives and axes left behind by their Polish neighbors and the bird catchers and sand miners of Balut before the ghetto was formed. They had even managed to hide the blades left by the ritual slaughterers, the *shokhtim*, when they were deported.

Each had acted alone, with no coordinated plan. Some still planned to scour the abandoned stables and dark cellars in hope of finding the rifles that the Jewish fighters had brought back from the final, futile battles of Kutno. True, after the defeat some of the fighters had immediately headed for the Vistula River, near Warsaw, where they'd joined others planning another attack in Kutno and Łowicz. But many of them, wounded in the fighting and driven by an impulse they could hardly understand, had returned to Balut and buried their bayonets and rifles. Maybe they were simply terrified of confronting the Germans again.

A group of these young Jewish fighters were now gathered together in Zelda's sickroom. They whispered to each other of events in other Polish ghettos—mysterious words flitted back and forth like the uncertain flight of swallows. There were warnings, followed by sighs and deep exhalations. Danger was lurking everywhere, even among presumed friends. Some of the men assembled around Zelda's bed had known each other a long time; they seemed capable of spending hours together in darkness, in silence. Others had wandered recently into the ghetto from the Aryan side, from "outside," and there was no telling if they were even Jewish or not. Sometimes, just as quickly, they would disappear again, driven by one of the coachmen toward the barbed-wire fence behind the cemetery. On very rare occasions, a Jew who'd escaped the Poznań labor camps would arrive in the ghetto, having braved the dangerous roads from the Warthegau. They would come armed with gruesome stories about the workers who'd been sent out of the ghetto. Through these newcomers, the young men and women of Balut discovered a vast, unfathomable world.

At first some resented the arrival of strange Jews who further reduced the meager ration of bread allotted to each. They didn't understand why these people had been thrown into the ghetto, and it took a long time to find a common language. They had their own ways of speaking and dressing, their own ways of gesturing. They looked as different as members of enemy tribes. But, by the fourth year of captivity, it had sunk in that they all shared a common fate. The danger hanging over them sealed their connection. In their desperate hope to outlast the hell of the ghetto, they found common ground, as ever when people are seized by the inexorable hand of fate. And so whoever they were, everyone who entered Zelda's sickroom seemed linked together by an invisible bond. They stole glances at each other and acknowledged every new face with a gentle nod.

Ever since Anton had hidden his violin under her bed, Zelda had sensed its presence beneath her body. She felt a strange passion for the instrument lying there in the darkness. Throughout long hours of fever and morbid visions, she could see behind closed eyelids the shining Stradivarius beckoning to her from its dark hiding place like a fantastic being. Sometimes she envisioned the wooden case as her own tomb. Sometimes, at night, when the house was silent but for the cry of a solitary night bird, she stroked the silken wood as if caressing a child asleep on her breast. She felt like the guardian of a secret, a hidden treasure preserved in the darkness like the distant reflection of heaven.

Like all who lay dying in the ghetto, Zelda spent hours conjuring up the faces of those who were already gone. In dreams and waking visions, she was visited by hazy silhouettes of family, neighbors, friends, and strangers. Called back from their untimely deaths, they stirred around her and sat down at the edge of her cot, their mouths agape like ghosts laughing unheard in dreams. Sometimes she would rise and go to meet them, dressed in her sheer, tattered nightgown. Once, it felt like her cot was rising toward the ceiling, lifted by dozens of arms. She floated above everyone in the room, feeling strangely euphoric. But then she'd been struck with terror that the violin would be stolen. The mysterious hands seemed to be bearing her far away from its secret hiding place, and she cried out in an echoing, inhuman voice. Then the hands had suddenly vanished, and she floated back down to the floor. She covered the violin case with a tattered blanket, relieved to discover that her secret had been kept.

Even later, when her fever fell, she imagined that hovering shadows surrounded her cot. She carried on long conversations with them at twilight, when the cool air would blow through the windows, filling her room with the light of distant stars. But the pale and airy shadows always dispersed again when she heard the quivering strings of the hidden Stradivarius beneath her. Then she listened for a long time to sounds that seemed to enter her bones, and the otherworldly faces escaped to distant corners of the room, where they merged with the flecks of light on the windowpanes and faded into the ghetto night.

✦

Vigdor stood still beside her, witnessing the final shudders of a life on its way out. He remembered their past life together, on the other side of the barbed wire. Now she was the only one left who connected him to that former life. For a moment he saw her as she had once been—her frail, slender neck, covered with soft down and, oh God, the secret allure of her slightly too-plump lower lip, filling him with desire. He closed his eyes, seized with regret. They had never consummated their desire.

As he approached her, his tears fell on the black boards of her cot. He felt ashamed of himself. The great tragedy that had struck the Jewish people, the death of his relatives, the unknown dangers weighing over the ghetto—none of that had made him cry like the sight of this girl's dying body in the half-light.

A ray of greenish light sliced through the darkness surrounding the cot. Vigdor could now see Zelda's head resting on a tiny straw pillow. It could hardly be called a human head—it was more like a skull, with decaying skin stretched over it. The few strands of white hair on Zelda's head resembled dried grass in an abandoned field. And where her neck should have been he saw only the outlines of her veins. Her closed eyelids fluttered as if trying to capture a distant dream woven by the oncoming darkness. Vigdor held his breath. A memory surfaced from his childhood—this was how he had imagined the dead would appear on the day of Resurrection, just before rising from the earth. Maybe all the dead would one day look exactly like Zelda did now, poised between life and death, preparing to rise from dust to eternal life.

As Vigdor sat on her bed, staring into the darkness, Anton Kraft rose and took hold of his violin. The hands that claimed the slender neck of the Stradivarius seemed to be illuminated from within by the radiance of old bones. As Anton tuned the violin, the circle of onlookers tightened around him. Long buried, the strings quivered like the lips of a mute who miraculously breaks into speech. It was dangerous to play music in the ghetto. Sounds leaked easily through cracks in the thin walls of the attic, and the roving wind could carry them to an enemy ear. The danger was great, and the onlookers screened him with their bodies to contain the sound, as a forest encloses the evening prayer of a solitary bird. A spring of water seemed to flow forth from the Stradivarius, singing like the waters of the mysterious Vltava under its innumerable bridges. Even now the Vltava was swathed in pink mist, each ripple reflecting the rays of the setting sun. Anton Kraft could see the bridges stretching across the sunlit river; he closed his eyes, as if to gather in the spots of brightness.

Other listeners had different visions. A former coachman from Balut, Mendele the invalid, returned to the blood and fire of the battlefield beyond Kutno. The last Polish soldiers were fleeing the banks of the Warta and dug into the soft turf of Kutno as they tried to stop the Germans. The night was clear. The stars seemed to hover just over their heads, and by their light, which pierced the darkness of the forest, he could see the German planes taking off. The soil of Kutno was soft and hot, half hidden under sand, stones, and human limbs. Mendele looked upward and fixed his eyes on the night sky, where the low stars dangled like ripe cherries.

By now the human form on the bed lay completely still. Gitele leaned against the bedpost and attempted to hold up her sister's heavy head. She tried to pry Zelda's eyelids open with her fingers, and a silent prayer stirred in Gitele's heart. She begged the stream of music to bring her sister back to life. She was waiting for the miracle. Then Zelda's body arched on the bunk and her lips pronounced a single word: *ma-ma . . .*

And Gitele saw their dead mother emerge from the shadows. A tiny, bent woman with a hollow Jewish face approached the cot. She bent over Zelda's body and whispered something in her ear. It must have been a word of encouragement, for Zelda seemed to stretch her legs as if meaning to get up and walk once again.

Then Anton stopped playing. The darkness in the room suddenly felt unbearably heavy. Gitele reached toward Vigdor with one arm, the other still propping up Zelda's head. Under her ragged bedclothes, Zelda's body was reduced to a tiny heap of bones. Moonlight cast white spots over the recesses of the room, as if a myriad of doves had landed on the dark wall and begun to flap their wings. Anton lowered his head in a gesture of farewell. Then, with closed eyes, he opened the black case, smoothed the soft layer of velvet, and enclosed the instrument in darkness.

4

Last Will and Testament

Vigdor bent over the wintry ground of the cemetery and picked up a fistful of dirt. Together with the other mourners, he threw it over Zelda's frozen body, barely concealed beneath its thin shroud. The dirt settled on her bony limbs like the last leaves of December.

The few people who came to Zelda's burial formed a semicircle of shadows around the open grave. Two gravediggers had wrapped their heads in torn shawls to protect against the biting cold rising off the bare fields. They were hastening to fill the pit like envoys of the Devil's army. Anton Kraft and Gitele stood closest to the grave's edge. Vigdor watched as tears froze on their pale cheeks and sparkled like pearls catching the light.

Vigdor had often accompanied victims of the ghetto to their final resting places. Some were relatives, some were people he barely knew. For his part, he refused to accept the deaths of so many Jews with the wearied resignation he saw in others. Many here were so cut off from the outside world that they thought a secret path to the gates of death was their only consolation. Surviving yet another night of hunger only made them sink deeper into gloom. But as he stood at the edge of Zelda's grave with the group that had been at her bedside the night before, he felt thankful that he'd met Gitele and fallen in with these silent men and women. Vigdor felt they were all bound together in their tremendous peril by a beautiful obscure power, and this power poured over him, too, like a soothing rain.

As he listened to the low voices of the gravediggers emptying their last shovelfuls of earth into the pit, he sensed his stomach tightening. He felt isolated once again and his gloomy thoughts returned. What were these Jews hoping for? After so many years of confinement, could they still envision their freedom? Wasn't every last remaining Jew here marked for death? There remained only a shapeless mass, united by fear and monotonous waiting. Where did they get their faith to carry on? Vigdor often thought it was simply a refusal to face the abyss—like reeds that tilted toward land to avoid the dark waters of a rushing stream. What is more dignified, he asked himself, to die in hope, though abandoned by God and the world, or to perish with your fist pounding against the heavens?

He turned to Anton Kraft, who now drew the Stradivarius case out from under his jacket. Why had this strange Czech Jew brought his violin to the cemetery? Was he going to offer it to Zelda as a keepsake in the cold ground, a consolation for all eternity? He turned to Gitele, who was standing next to Anton. She met his gaze through a veil of swirling snow. Although she was weighed down with sadness, her delicate face, framed by a black scarf, looked beautiful to Vigdor. All of her prayers and hidden desires seemed revealed in her hungry green eyes. Standing there in front of Zelda's rigid body lying in the grave, Vigdor felt that he loved Gitele with the same doomed passion he'd felt for her sister. He and Gitele seemed to share the vague feeling that Zelda had brought them together by some unwritten last will and testament. Why shouldn't the dead bequeath to the living the passion that burned in their blood? Zelda's love had not disappeared with her ravaged body, but continued to flow through her sister's veins.

Vigdor and Gitele both stared at the tiny mound of dirt near the pit, which was flecked with a crown of glistening snowflakes. He felt ashamed to be thinking of his own desires. Yet everyone yearned for consolation, some reprieve from the loneliness of the world. The wind stirred up the snow, and Vigdor's eyes drifted from the grave to the mist-shrouded world beyond the ghetto walls.

As the mourners left the burial ground, the bluish haze of dusk enveloped the ghetto. No lights could be seen within the ramshackle wooden houses. Ever since the Soviet tanks had begun approaching the eastern banks of the Vistula, lighting lamps had been banned in the ghetto. Amid the winding alleys you could sometimes spot the shadow of a Jew, flitting in the darkness like the wings of a startled bird. A battle seemed underway between the white snowflakes descending on the ghetto and the darkness rising from below. Sometimes victory seemed to be on the side of the light, sometimes darkness prevailed. Beyond the ghetto walls, cries went up near the German guard posts like the nervous howling of wolves. The whistling of bullets could also be heard through the whirlwind of snow; somewhere a Jew tumbled to the ground, his blood staining the whiteness.

Once they had left the burial ground, Gitele leaned toward Vigdor.

"You'll be coming to our house, Vigdor. Won't you?"

She gently touched his sleeve and let her hands slide down his arm.

"Please, please come and see us. It's unbearably sad without Zelda . . . I'll make us a cup of coffee, nice and hot."

Then she hesitated a moment and added, "But we don't have any sugar. Can you drink bitter coffee?"

How could she say such a thing? Her doubts made him feel unbearably sad and he kept silent. Months had passed since anything sweet had touched his lips. Did she imagine he was different from the shadowy masses, a foreigner in the ghetto?

As they stood facing each other on the road, Anton gazed at them from a distance. He hadn't noticed Vigdor before, and he marveled at the sudden intimacy between them.

Gitele turned and saw his surprise.

"Don't worry, we can trust him. He's coming to see us. He'll be one of us. One of *us*. Don't you see, Anton?"

But Anton was no longer listening. He turned and hurried away, his wooden clogs clunking along the broken pavement. Gitele and Vigdor watched as he disappeared into the twilight. The last thing they saw was the Stradivarius case slung over his shoulder, at rest among the dancing threads of his tattered coat. Gitele pulled Vigdor in closer to her, as they walked together down an alleyway through the falling snow. The darkness led them through empty courtyards to the lonely room that death had visited only the day before.

✦

As they stepped through the door, the darkness was so thick that Vigdor had to steady himself against the wall. Gitele guided him in silence, laying her warm hands on his shoulders. She led him to the cot. Then she threw off her scarf and shook the snow from her hair with such quick and agile gestures that Vigdor imagined an enchanted bird had been released into the room. She said something he couldn't catch and stuffed a fistful of twigs into the stove. They sparkled as if glowing with a myriad of orange pupils. A gust of wind sucked the flame into the chimney, swallowing the fire as soon as it was lit. All the while Vigdor was sitting on the very bed where Zelda had expired the day before. The last dress she wore lay underneath him.

Vigdor felt a great weariness descend on him after the ordeal of the burial. He sank into morbid thoughts, as Gitele busied herself with the stove. The fire struggled to come to life, the flames sputtering in the wind and casting wild, dancing shadows on the wall. Beyond the fence of the ghetto, far to the east, Vigdor could see the moon surrounded by shimmering constellations. Finally, Vigdor heard the girl pouring liquid into a cup. She joined him on the bed and they drank the steamy, bitter coffee in silence. Each sip warmed their icy blood, and the darkness outside seemed to dissipate before their eyes, giving way to a strange gray luminosity. The moonlight played on the ghetto courtyard outside the window.

"It's lucky that we ran into one another, isn't it, Vigdor?"

"Yes, that morning on the bridge."

"Zelda kept talking about you."

He widened his eyes, surprised she was being so direct. Zelda's emaciated body, buried only hours earlier, appeared suddenly before him. He saw her, with an almost blinding clarity, leaning toward them and smiling. Her long hands were reaching out.

"Gitele, what's the point of talking about the dead now? What's the point?"

"She wanted to see you so badly. But you, you never came. Why not? Why didn't you ever visit us, Vigdor?"

In spite of her critical tone, Vigdor felt in Gitele's closeness the promise of renewed joy, the return of vanished dreams. He began in a low voice to tell her about the early days of the ghetto. His wife had committed a terrible act; it was unhuman, un-Jewish. Unable to accept being condemned to captivity in the ghetto, she'd gotten her hands on a lethal dose of cyanide pills. For herself and their child. It happened just as they were building the first black fence. They couldn't save his wife, but the child survived. Yet not long afterward she too died—of hunger. And what had become of him? He'd sunk deeper and deeper into darkness, into the oblivion of ghetto life. He waited. But what *had* he been waiting for all these years?

The girl was silent for a long time. Then he heard her weeping in short, strangled sobs. Her grief-stricken voice pierced the silence like a narrow blade.

"Zelda loved you so much, she really did. And you loved her. It was a long time ago, I know. She told me everything."

"Gitele, what's the point? What's the point of going over it?"

"But you don't even know her last wish. I need to tell you."

"Her last wish?"

His body tensed up and he grabbed the girl's hands. They felt cold and as hard as glass.

"Zelda told me to pass on a message from her. It was her last wish. I'm so glad fate brought us together before she died, and now that she's dead . . ."

They remained silent a moment, watching the flames through the cracks in the stove. A triumphant gust of wind shook the windows. A thicker darkness seemed to rise from the floor around the stove, moving and spreading like a black cloud. The reflection of the moon wavered in the window, and large snowflakes clung to the panes of glass like mute white symbols in a lost language.

"She was constantly saying your name. It was always 'Vigdor, Vigdor.' She even wanted me to go out and find you, so you could come and be one of us. You are *worthy* of it, that's what she kept saying. You're worthy . . ."

"Worthy?" he repeated softly, surprised by her secretive tone.

"She kept telling me you were *worthy* to be with us—to be with people who didn't want to be slaughtered like sheep by the Germans, trampled under their feet like grass. She kept asking people if they knew you or had heard of you. And now her final wish has come true.

"Come on, let's go—over *there*, to the group with the radio. Maybe there will be good news for us, for the ghetto. You realize, Vigdor, that up until now there have only been about sixty people in the whole ghetto, sixty people in the *whole* ghetto with the strength and the faith, who are ready for anything? Maybe there will be more. There *need* to be more. This was her last wish. It's as if people have been paralyzed by fear, fear of the Germans, fear of hunger, fear of dying. Why should we, the last ones here, waste our lives? Do we want to betray everyone who's already died?"

Burning with an inner fire, he squeezed the girl's hands. Not a word slipped out of his clenched throat, yet his heart was pounding with the sudden reawakening of the passion for justice, which he had long ago presumed dead. Gitele seemed like a shining menorah placed miraculously in his path by the hand of fate.

"And Zelda told me more. She told me that when she died, I should find you and tell you her last wishes. She told me you would protect me and love me just as you'd loved her. She said you honor life and you'll wash away the shame of all our dead."

She cradled his neck with her hands and pulled her face toward him. As her hair pressed against his cheek in the darkness, Vigdor breathed in a sweetness uncorrupted by the ghetto. He closed his eyes and tried to form words, but his lips were stopped by the sudden, burning touch of her mouth. The feeling lasted only a moment, but it jolted him with the force of lightning. Long-buried desires sprang back to life in his starving body. He held her warm shoulders, and, in the dim light reflecting off the falling snow, he again felt her mouth hungrily seeking his lips. For a moment he was gripped with shame, a devastating feeling of self-disgust. Had she already forgotten Zelda's funeral, hours earlier? Were they not sitting this very moment in the room where she had died? Couldn't they still hear her final agonized weeping, her prayers echoing in the room? But this fugitive memory of loss only led him back to the present moment in the darkness of the room.

Meanwhile blue-tinged snow was piling up outside, and the howling wind was lashing against the walls. This young woman whom he barely knew seemed transformed by remote powers. Maybe these powers had been summoned forth from the open grave they had stood beside a few hours earlier; maybe they had been swept into her by the constant presence of death. But there, in the dark room with a deathbed in the corner, these two shadowy figures felt the reawakening of human love. They were prepared to join together in a strange new bond, born of darkness and death. He held her hands and she let herself be guided like a child. As he lifted her, a shudder ran through her body, and he cloaked her in Zelda's last remaining dress before laying her down on the bed. She held his neck tightly, drawing him toward her in anxious anticipation. Suddenly a breath seemed to blow past their faces, as if from Zelda herself, and Vigdor felt he was looking straight into her dead sister's shining eyes, lighting up the room like stars across the heavens. With tightened lips, they listened to the sweet breath of death, letting themselves be borne away, shepherded by the scattered light of the stars.

5

In the Darkness

Two days later, just past midnight, two shadowy figures moved through the western district of the ghetto. They stole across the wooden bridge and passed the crumbling vaults and cracked headstones of the old cemetery. Under cover of darkness, they arrived at a desolate snowy courtyard.

For months now, the western side of the ghetto had been "cleansed" of its Jews. Even the Germans rarely entered this section. Strangely, even *they* felt safer among crowds of Jews than in these abandoned streets. It was exceedingly dangerous for a Jew to walk down the empty roadways and past the dilapidated houses. Shots often rang out at night from the guard posts near the rail factory. But the danger lurking here could not deter those who kept the spark of Jewish courage alive in their hearts. And now two meager shadows flitted across the courtyard, driven by a single desire: *to hear* news from the outside world, the free world beyond these walls, and to bring words of comfort to the starving men and women inside the ghetto.

Vigdor and Gitele strode along a narrow path, their footsteps leaving black trails in the snow behind them. They stopped to catch their breath at the entrance of an abandoned house. As they removed their scarves to shake off the snow, they turned to each other and embraced with a long kiss. The lovers' warm breath rose along the cold walls of the musty-smelling, cobweb-covered entrance. They wrapped their scarves back around their heads and squeezed through a crack in the walls, treading lightly like skittish deer. Since their first night together, they had been united by a strong bond, not merely the bond of their new love, but of their devotion to a common cause, which sent them on nightly forays into the deserted ghetto, and now to a long-awaited appointment with the basement radio operator.

They held hands as they climbed over a low, broken-down fence. The snow had just stopped, and the bone-white moonshine of the Polish winter cut through the clouds, filling the courtyard with silvery light. They turned to each other in the sudden glow and shuddered. Looking over the rows of empty houses, Vigdor imagined he was among ruins of desecrated tombs. He pictured grotesque, grimacing faces in the cracked windows rattling in their frames. Suddenly a pair of eyes flashed out at them through a low window. Vigdor and Gitele stared in wonder at the tiny spheres reflecting a gleaming red and green. These could not possibly be human eyes, more likely those of an abandoned dog or cat. Maybe they were the eyes of Zelda's ghost, which had stayed with them since their first night together. Or maybe it was a living Jew after all, stranded in the empty ghetto, eyes sunken and hollowed-out by starvation.

Clutching hands, they slowly approached the house, listening at the windows. A heavy stench blew from inside, doubtless a rotting corpse in one of the rooms. They lit a match and followed the dim glow in the direction of the unearthly smell. When they crossed the threshold into a small room, they again saw those strange pupils floating just above the ground, flashing red and green. Now they understood: the eyes belonged to a dog, pacing around a human corpse. The dog pointed its snout at the body, which was naked from the waist up, its bare yellowing toes stretched out like the spread hands of a holy man performing the Priestly Blessing. A thin sheet of snow had blown through the window onto its chest and head, which hung limply to one side. The dog crouched over the corpse's feet and seemed prepared to remain there a long time. It lifted its eyes and stared intently at the two intruders. It looked almost regretful, as if suddenly aware of the sordidness of the whole scene. Still holding hands, Gitele and Vigdor gazed in horror as the dog let out a tortured lament over the corpse.

Quickly surveying the room, they discovered a torn curtain in the shadows and covered the corpse from head to toe, all the while avoiding its gaping eyes. The dog strayed from the body and lay at the feet of the new guests, rubbing its back on the floor. Vigdor searched in vain for something of value in the corners of the room; then he rushed outside into the courtyard.

Left alone, Gitele sat down on a low bed, cradling the emaciated dog. She knew what Vigdor was doing outside; they were going to bury the stranger. Sitting with the dog on her knees, she began to cry, and it was as if both of them, Gitele and the dog, were suddenly uttering the same low moan in a single voice. Her tears seemed to comfort the dog, who settled into her lap with an unexpected tenderness. Gitele began thinking about Zelda and the ordeal of her burial. As the dog's panting grew louder, she felt warm breaths on her knees. Both kept their eyes fixed on the heap of bones before them. The windows rattled in the wind, and the light of a few lonely, scattered stars shone into the room, bringing a strange feeling of peace.

Soon Vigdor returned, and they lifted the body, which was heavy as a stone, seemingly reluctant to leave the floor. There was no hint of whether it had been an old or young man. They discovered a ragged prayer shawl under the corpse. With their last strength, they dragged the body to the narrow pit that Vigdor had carved out of the ground in the tiny brick-lined courtyard. They carefully laid their burden in the grave as the moon flooded the courtyard in a river of light. Vigdor's lips murmured the barely remembered Kaddish. The dog encircled the snowy mound several times before stretching out and resting its head between its paws.

Vigdor and Gitele hurried out of the courtyard, fearful that they would be seen. They thought they heard distant voices piercing the night's silence. As they squeezed again through the wall, they turned around to look one final time at the mound of snow covering the makeshift grave. Once again the dog's eyes shone up at them. This time they seemed wider, almost human in their awareness. Vigdor and Gitele raised their heads and gazed into the night sky. They understood now that the dog's pupils were reflecting distant lights, shining into the darkness. They were the lights of God's tiny, comforting stars, flickering over a walled-in realm of death.

6

On the Other Side

A few days later, a peasant drove his sleigh at dusk through the newly fallen snow on the road to Łagiewniki. Beyond the snow-topped hills, the horizon was tinted with a rosy glow. The Polish winter had spread a delicate veil of frost over the landscape as if casting a spell. Silence reigned over the open fields and orchards, where bare fruit trees seemed to stretch up their arms to support the heavy sky. The fluttering wings of a few scattered blackbirds flashed from time to time among the hedges. They were taking refuge for the night in the forest, where the crowns of the towering pines jutted above the frosty mist.

As the sleigh began its steep climb, the horse began breathing loudly. White foam gathered at the edges of its mouth as it bobbed its head from side to side, gazing at the huts and wooden granaries buried in the snow along the road. Eager as it was to find a warm stable filled with hay and straw, the horse always returned to the snowy path, pounding the earth with a clatter of hooves. A wide tarpaulin covered the back of the sleigh, where three boxes jostled against one another. Wrapped in a sheepskin coat and wearing a fur cap, the peasant was rambling on constantly to his horse. As the sleigh slid over the lonely road, his words cut through the icy sky, echoing across the fields.

The peasant's long mustache was twirled up at the tips. It shimmered in the frost, stiff as two horns. He kept up his constant banter with the horse, speaking to the animal's backside while looking up occasionally at the pink sky that hung lower and lower over the snowfields.

For several years now, since Poland's tragic September of '39, Antoni had hardly been able to leave home or travel out on his own. His tiny plot of land, his farm outside Głowno, his sick wife—who had been bedridden for twenty years and still wouldn't die—all of this kept him stuck, as if nailed to the ground. It was so difficult nowadays that people everywhere preferred to stay at home or on their farms, rather than face the unstable world with its countless evils. He had once left his village—but that was only at the very beginning. Now, even if all the saints in heaven suddenly descended and told him to do otherwise, would he have the courage? He would wait—such a terrible state of affairs couldn't last forever. And if he was the only person in his whole village who *could* do something, wasn't that a sign that everyone else had lost all connection with God and the Son of God? Only Satan, the Antichrist himself, could turn this world into such hell, wasn't that right? But who was this damned devil, huh? *Onward, hey yo!* Just a few more steps now and we'll be there, a few more steps . . .

As the sleigh reached the peak of the hill, the horse sunk deeper into the snow, which was tinged with blue under the darkening sky.

What else could we have done? They all just stood there, wringing their hands, everyone in the Jewish quarter. The tailor, the innkeeper, even the rabbi. Such a clever people, our Żydzi, and then all of a sudden, they all lose their heads. *Oy vey! We're doomed! Mama, Papa! Co to jest? How will it end? The Germans are forming a ghetto. What will happen in the ghetto?* Nobody seemed to understand anything, though they probably understood all too well, which made them burst into tears. And what hurt all the more was that we good people, we God-fearing peasants, we stepped aside, hands on hips, doing nothing. True, nobody liked to be close to another's tragedy. But how can you stand by and watch and do nothing? All they were asking for, the Żydzi, was a wagon ride. They wanted to get to Warsaw, maybe Łódź, maybe it would be better there. But no one moved a muscle, the sons of bitches. The Germans, they said, confiscate everything they find along the road, carts, horses, they send them all to Prussia. Who wanted to go out on the road with such a risk? It was true, they'd always been good neighbors, and they were no fools, these Żydzi, but who wanted to risk their neck? And if it had been the other way around? If *we'd* had to go into the ghetto, not them, what would they have done, these clever people? Gone with us? But why did the Germans pick on the Jews? Oh Lord Jesus, sweet Lord Jesus, what a sad world this is. What hell on earth! *Hey yo!*

Antoni's head was getting foggy. He shouldn't have had those two glasses of brandy before setting off. True, he'd been dragging himself through the cold for more than two hours. No, actually, his head was clear, clearer than ever. But why, then, were so many little black-haired Jews suddenly dancing around his sleigh? Jews with thick beards, some hanging all the way down to the ground, others short and stringy like an old goat's; and why were they all blocking the road? Look at that one, with long side curls and a caftan, lying in the middle of the road, waiting for the horse to trample him. And what about that other one trying to grab the reins? His face was concealed by his beard, leaving only his sunken Jewish eyes visible. Such strange cries from his mouth—he was about to leap into the sleigh! And now the road was covered in darkness, and groans were coming from under the snow: *Hey there! Hey!*

"In the name of the Father, the Son . . . !"

Standing up in his sleigh, Antoni crossed himself and frantically pulled in the reins. In the sudden stillness, he rubbed his eyes and looked around at the fields. The dark little Jews had all vanished in the snow. His horse was breathing hard—above him God's stars were shining peacefully as if in a distant canopy. He lifted his eyes, surprised to see how many stars had risen. In the distance he could still see rosy streaks in the sky. A line of winter birds heading for the forest left a silken rustle of wings in the air. They flew higher and higher toward the pink clouds, as if trying to reach the glittering stars.

Now he remembered everything as if it were yesterday. But how many years had it been? Maybe four years, four whole years. Mrs. Moszek had been constantly trying to stuff a tiny package into his pocket: *Take, Antoni, my friend . . . Please take. Take these jewels, take all. Get your horse and bring us away from here, to anyplace . . .*

to big city. Please, Antoni, take our jewelry—it's good for you. But even if they'd offered all the earth's treasures, would he have taken them? So many years living side by side. Yes, they were Jews . . . But so what? Was it their fault they were born Jewish? Now it had been four years since he'd seen a single Jew, not in town, not in the village. Even he, Antoni himself, could have been born a Jew. What then? The same *Mama, Papa, Oy vey*? No! Keep your tiny package, Mrs. Moszek, you'll need it; bad days are coming! And tomorrow morning, before dawn, we'll load the cart and leave for Łódź! *Hey yo!*

Traveling down the road, among these slumbering snowy fields, Antoni now remembered dragging the heavy load in his wagon. They'd made it all the way to the city limits, and once again Mrs. Moszek had tried to smuggle a gold ring into his hand. *Take it for your troubles,* she'd said. When he'd refused yet again, she'd fallen upon him and kissed his arms and shoulders. Then they'd said goodbye, first she, then her two daughters, and finally old man Moszek himself. Antoni had never seen Jews giving kisses. All of a sudden, the old man had thrown his arms around him and kissed him on his mustache, a warm, wet kiss from an old Jew. Then they'd walked off down the road toward the cemetery. Oh, how terrible that the Germans had built a ghetto next to a cemetery, not a good omen. Mrs. Moszek had turned around and stared back at Antoni a long time. Antoni again made the sign of the cross in the air for them. May Jesus protect you, since your Jewish God has abandoned you!

Hey, yo!

The horse refused to continue his snowy trek and came to a sudden stop in the middle of the road. By now night had deepened—an immense tapestry unfurled overhead, embroidered with stars. Antoni got down from his sleigh and moved in the darkness alongside his horse. He tried to warm the shivering creature, regretting his decision to visit the bell ringer on such a night. Better to wait for the cold snap to end. But after getting a letter like that one, how could he put off his trip? Nikodem had managed to send off a message, saying he badly needed potatoes, at least five sacks, and just as many cabbages. That should be enough for the rest of winter. How long had it been since his last delivery of potatoes, turnips, and cabbages? Antoni felt like it had been just after the first snowfall—now it was barely a month after Christmas. How could one man eat so many potatoes and cabbages?

The peasant climbed back into his seat, pleased to see the road was beginning its downward turn. Far off at the bottom of the hill, he could make out a flickering orange dot; it was the window of the little wooden Church of Saint Francis in Łagiewniki. He would still have to pass the Kaczmarek Inn, which worried him. Anything could happen there. It was always full of Germans, Volksdeutsche from western Ukraine and guards who manned the posts outside the ghetto, near the wire fence. Then there were always Poles as well, many of them suspicious-looking characters who must have had some kind of business with the Germans. The guards would stop at the inn for their beer, though they had to cross a large field to get there, nearly a kilometer. They didn't mind the trip. You couldn't get a beer on the north side of the ghetto.

The Kaczmarek Inn had sprung up all at once, just as the Germans were setting up their strange Jewish quarter. The small wooden houses, scattered like beehives, had been abandoned as the peasants fled into the interior of the country. Then the Germans took over the shacks, and the sandy fields around the Jewish quarter became a deserted no-man's-land. Nobody knew what the Germans were up to. Peasant wagons became rarer along the road to Łagiewniki and German trucks more common, rushing past the northern fields behind the ghetto with an evil whirring sound.

Only the Kaczmarek family had remained behind. They held firm to their red-brick house near the hill where the church spire poked up toward the sky. Long before the war, old Jan Kaczmarek had a motto that he repeated to his family on his deathbed: "If you want to earn your bread, live near the Jews!" His sons, Adam and Stefan, and his daughter, Marta, lived by this dictum. Over the years, they spent less and less time in the barn, stopped working the land, and even neglected the garden behind their house. But they carried on all sorts of business with the Jews traveling the roads between Łódź and Warsaw with their carts stuffed with merchandise. The Kaczmareks bought, sold, and traded anything you could name: peat and loam, wood, leather, wheat, cotton, wool, jewelry, horses, cows, and pigs. A constant bellowing and grunting of cattle emanated from behind the Kaczmarek house—farm dogs were constantly running in and out of the courtyard, barking and snarling at the other animals. In the front room, Marta would serve *bimber* that the family distilled in a back room, along with Jewish-style fish and roast goose. When the heavy snows piled up, Jewish wagon drivers, brokers, and traders heading to market would stop for the night, sometimes staying for several days. They would snore away in the first-floor rooms, lying on large multicolored pillows, and when they got up, they would quickly mutter their prayers in a corner of the room decorated with crucifixes and images of the saints. Marta enjoyed having Jews around. She enjoyed their nervous reactions when her bare arms and heavy breasts rubbed against them. She would tug at their leather coats to get their attention, pat their bearded cheeks, drink schnapps with them, and breathe her unfamiliar womanly aromas into their Jewish faces.

But as soon as war broke out, the Jews had disappeared, mostly locked up in the ghetto, and the Kaczmarek house had gone silent. Trading with merchants came to a halt. If it hadn't been for the old man's motto to always live near the Jews, the family would have left with the other Poles. True, there weren't any Jews to be seen, but everything could change again in an instant.

And then, when the Germans completed the fence around the ghetto on the northern edge of the city, the Kaczmareks' room and halls were crowded once again—but now with other sorts of people. And trade resumed, not with the Jews themselves, but with the possessions they had left behind in the towns and villages. Furs, clothing, shoes, and jewelry piled up in the rooms where Jewish merchants had once slept. It wasn't quite as lively as before, but once again Marta poured brandy and sliced up pieces of roast pork as she counted up the reichsmarks she collected from the Volksdeutsche, smugglers, and other sorts of suspicious characters who stopped in on their way to God knows where. Once she even hid a Jew who'd fled the ghetto, concealing him in an empty sauerkraut barrel in the stable. He hardly looked like a Jew at all. In exchange for the few hours she let him hide, he gave her a golden watch, set with diamonds. She wore it to this day, though the watch had stopped long ago. Hanging in the bedroom filled with objects taken from Jewish homes was a large portrait of old Jan Kaczmarek. His blue eyes gazed out on all the amassed wealth. As Marta moved about the room, she couldn't help looking up at her old father. She could almost read his lips repeating his dictum. You couldn't say he'd been wrong. *Live near the Jews*. Even if it meant living near a ghetto. Even a ghetto.

News of the Kaczmarek Inn traveled far beyond the borders of the Łagiewniki region. Dubious characters of all kinds flocked there from every surrounding town and village that had previously housed a Jewish family. They brought whatever they'd pillaged from the deserted houses, items Jews had left in hopes of retrieving after the war. It was like a secret black river flowing from many tributaries, swelling to a flood, and pouring into the red-brick Kaczmarek house. When the Germans arrived, people who had once worked for Jews continued to live on their former employers' wealth. These Jews, now behind barbed wire, were paying them with their old clothes, household wares, and hidden jewels. The only ones who kept away from the Kaczmarek Inn were those who could still eke out a living from the land, or from some kind of handicraft, or who simply wanted to avoid getting swept up in the sordid mess.

Antoni knew all about these changes. He worried more and more as he approached the inn. What would stop them from coming out and asking why he was carrying so many potatoes? Where was he bringing them and why so late at night? Maybe for a Jew somewhere? He tried to stop his horse, but the sleigh was already sliding down the hill in front of the inn. He could hear the raucous voices, mixed with the tinny wail of a harmonica. As he watched in the darkness, the inn door flung open, releasing a cloud of smoke that hung over the road like a white rope. The sleigh careened to the left and slid under a thicket of frozen pines. As the horse led them down a steep slope, Antoni crossed himself, clenched his fists, and hissed through his teeth.

"You're a bunch of sinners and you're all going to hell! You're sinners! Sinners! Sinners! Sinners!"

At the bottom of the hill, the pine grove thinned out. Antoni stopped between patches of snow. He got off his sleigh and walked the remaining ten paces to the church, his heavy boots sinking deep into the mud. A candle flashed from a tiny window; it was the bell ringer of Łagiewniki, waiting up for him. For hours he had been sitting at the window, anxiously scanning the landscape, listening alertly like a forest animal. He could already smell the season changing. The Polish spring was rising from the mud, blowing through the low-hanging pine branches. Nikodem could hear drops of melting snow, heralding the great thaw. Deep in the forest, under a leaden sky, sheets of ice could be heard cracking like the secret, pious song of imprisoned birds.

7

The Bell Ringer

Nikodem Załucki, the bell ringer of Łagiewniki, was a man in the autumn of his years. Since his youth, he had served at the little church of Saint Francis of Assisi. Now the church had sunk into the earth. Its wooden facade was worm-eaten and partly covered with moss. Two black bell towers stood on the roof like the wooden cubes from a pair of phylacteries. Red-copper bells hung inside each tower, their long, braided cords dangling to the ground. A sloping field, usually blanketed by fog, led from the church to the northern part of the city where the ghetto lay. From the churchyard, you could see the ruddy walls of the ghetto cemetery, the scattered mounds of dirt—and sometimes crowds of Jews digging pits, the final resting places for their dead.

Now that the Germans had destroyed the surrounding houses and resettled the peasants in nearby villages, the church looked like an abandoned ruin. Mournful saints gazed out from dusty stained-glass windows at the desolate fields, the broken-down houses, and the brick walls of the cemetery. Their heads, bowed in submission, were crowned with shining halos; their interwoven beards resembled those of old Jews. Some of the saints carried shepherd sticks; many wore colorful tunics. They appeared eager to leave their window frames and set off on a long journey, sticks in hand. When the evening bells echoed across the fields and the sun set in the Łagiewniki Forest, their weary faces would glow in the dim light, as if they belonged to souls wandering through purgatory.

It was only years later that people learned why Saint Francis's church had been permitted to remain standing. It was thanks to the Kaczmarek Inn, and especially Marta's intervention, that the Germans had not destroyed it. She'd explained that it didn't block the view of the German guards, so what was the use in destroying it? With or without it, they could easily spot the slightest movement of a shadow in or out of the ghetto.

The houses north of the ghetto had been leveled, but scattered orchards still remained near the half-sunken ruins of the foundations. In the springtime, ancient apple and pear trees and hundred-year-old Polish oaks would come into bloom. Birds would build nests in the overhanging branches. All year long, stray dogs watched over mounds of bricks that had once been a furnace or a stable—or rummaged hungrily among collapsed chimneys and exposed cellars where rainwater collected in dark pools. They pricked up their ears whenever suspicious noises rang out—noises from the ghetto or from the distant black steeples of the Church of Saint Francis. It always seemed a novelty for the dogs: the piercing sound of copper bells, echoing through the air as if determined to shatter the sky.

And though people no longer lived anywhere near the church, the bell ringer never let a day go by without entering the courtyard, clutching the ropes with both hands, and letting the copper bells ring for a good long while. He did it exactly as he had since the old days, before Father Jankowski had been taken by the Germans and his bones buried who knows where. Every time the bells sounded in the vacant fields around the ghetto, it was as if old Nikodem was uttering a solitary, stubborn prayer. He knew no one would come to Mass, and the echo of the bells would resound through distant pine groves only to sink unheeded in dark-green lakes. Still, he rang the bells as if multitudes depended on it.

Sometimes he awoke in the middle of the night and sat at the edge of his bed, listening to a wailing voice on the other side of the ghetto wall. Then he would reach for the Holy Scriptures to drive away the cries with passages known to console solitary old men. Maybe the Jews on the other side were burying their dead at precisely this hour, and this was the lamentation of their prayer leader. Sometimes he would ring the bells, hoping to provide fitting accompaniment for the ghetto funeral. He imagined he was summoning the dead saints of Poland from the depths of the forest, along with a procession of priests, farmers, craftsmen, shepherds, and, leading them all, Jews in mournful black frock coats, their beards thick as a monk's. He imagined them all in the church courtyard, listening to the bells' secret message, perhaps an incantation against death.

When the cries from the ghetto were too much for him, he shook the bells even harder to exorcise the agonized wailing of the Jews. Sometimes a piercing metallic sound would rise above the low echo of the tolling copper, as if a hidden god inside the bells could no longer contain its sorrow. Still the voices from the ghetto would not stop. Then he would pull and pull on the rope until the night clouds dissipated and the clear face of the moon illuminated the church towers. And when the bell ringer finally dropped his rope, the lamentations seemed as close as if from a wounded doe at the edge of the forest. Could it be their holy mother Rachel, risen from the grave, weeping over her Jewish children?

More than once, the clanging of the bells lured German soldiers out of the inn. They wondered at the loud noise, so late at night. Was it a sign of revolt? A signal for the Jews to rise up? Drunken Germans would come running through the streets, shooting at the church spires. Some aimed at the moon itself. Gradually the clanging would die down. As the last echoes reverberated on the northern hills, the bell ringer would look up and imagine the moon itself had been wounded in the melee. He'd think he could make out a gray teardrop on its face, turning bloodred against the dawning sky.

Nikodem spent whole days kneeling on an old rug before the altar, his gaze fixed on the figure of Jesus, nailed to a wooden cross. The body was so long that its feet almost touched the floor. Nikodem sometimes thought the figure wasn't nailed to the cross at all, but rather floated in the air, arms spread wide to embrace the faithful. As he sat bowed low to the ground, the bell ringer could easily touch the twisted toes with his lips. This part of the church was cold and dim like an underground mausoleum; the oil lamps in the corners had long ago stopped burning. Behind the crucifix, there was a smaller, darker figure made of painted plaster, a statue of Saint Francis of Assisi. His outstretched right arm had been severed at the elbow by a stray German bullet that once flew through a church window. Nikodem considered the severed limb, with its yellowing fingers, a sacred relic; he kept it on the table, under a thin cloth. Sometimes he caressed it while whispering a prayer. Under one of the fingernails of this strange relic a mysterious red spot was visible, like a speck of blood.

To this day, the bell ringer could not forget the moment the Jew arrived. It was late at night when gunshots rang out from near the ghetto walls. Suddenly a strange figure appeared at the entrance to the church, silent in his ragged coat, his eyes begging for mercy. He had a full head of thick hair and weary Jewish eyes. He reminded Nikodem of Saint Francis himself. Although it was foolish to hide him, the bell ringer was so moved by the pious look in the Jew's eyes that he led the stranger through a trapdoor in front of the altar into the cellar. Nikodem spent all night kneeling on the carpet that covered the secret passage, staring at the figure on the cross.

"Son of our Heavenly Father! Thou also comest from the seed of Abraham and David. Save this poor man! Thou art also a Jew . . . Save thy brother! Save him!"

And then, who knows, maybe a miracle happened. How else could he explain it? The Germans searched everywhere in the dark courtyard; they entered the church and found the bell ringer kneeling before the altar. Eyeing him suspiciously, they turned and gazed for a long time at the wooden figure on the cross. They walked slowly around the crucifix, examining it closely, even touching it, as if convinced that the fugitive had transformed himself by some devious Jew magic into the dead man nailed to his wooden cross.

And what the bell ringer did the next day—with the strange man in the cellar, giving no sign of life—this tormented him still. There had been no other way to save him, and it would have been worse to let him die. What would he have done with the body? He was certain the man would die from the cold. A white frost was rolling in from the forest. It would have been very dangerous to lead the man out of the church. God will forgive his sin—God will forgive him for giving the man in the cellar two bottles filled with holy wine. After all, the bottles had stood there untouched for years. But what a great sin to defile the blood of Christ!

From that night the Germans had kept an ever-closer watch over the church. Not a day passed without one of them coming over from the bar. As soon as he heard boots outside, Nikodem would rush to the tiny rug, kneel before the altar, and begin saying his prayers aloud. He would keep it up until the sound of the footsteps died away in the distance. Twice a day, under cover of darkness, Nikodem would roll up the worn rug, lift a tiny latch, and let down into the dark opening a plate of potatoes still in their skins. A bony yellow hand would slowly rise through the darkness, and then quickly snatch the plate. It was like somebody's hand rising from the grave on the day of Resurrection. To the bell ringer it felt like discovering a lost soul in the void. One time the cold hand grabbed his fingers and refused to let go; Nikodem was terrified. Another time he thought that the severed arm of Saint Francis had somehow found its way into the dark cellar. Nikodem rushed to his little table and lifted the cloth. No, Saint Francis's hand was still there, motionless in its suspended dream. But as he stared at his treasured relic, the fingers seemed to move, relaxing their joints as if readying to shake someone's hand.

8

The Stranger

It was soon clear to Nikodem that the man hiding in the cellar was not a runaway from the ghetto. There was no question he was a Jew, but he was from somewhere else, far away. When things quieted down around the church, the bell ringer ventured into the cellar, where he found the stranger lying in the corner like a crumpled old sack. The room smelled of mildew; it was cold enough to see his breath. For a long time Nikodem tried to make out the stranger's face in the darkness; finally, he reached out and found his cold, bony fingers. Though they could hardly see each other, their touch brought a sudden feeling of fellowship. The stranger asked in a low hoarse voice if he had the pleasure of addressing Pan Nikodem, the bell ringer of Łagiewniki. No sooner had the stunned old man answered, than the stranger pulled him closer and quickly whispered his story. He came from the forest. He brought greetings—greetings from the bell ringer's son, Tadeusz. Hearing his son's name on the stranger's lips, the bell ringer embraced him and began to weep.

Then the stranger handed Nikodem a crumpled note. In the dim light that filtered into the cellar from the church nave above, he could see clearly that it was written in Tadeusz's hand. "My dear Father," it said in uneven letters. "I am alive and well. Do everything possible for this man. He is my friend. He is on an important mission. Please take care of yourself, dear Father. We will see each other again one day."

Later, by the light of a tiny oil lamp, Nikodem reread his son's note, as he would again and again over the following weeks. This was the first word he'd had from his son since the Germans had arrived. There were rumors that Tadeusz had joined others in the Parczew Forest. As for the "important mission," the bell ringer heard more about it the next day, but still the precise details eluded him. The stranger had to get *inside* the ghetto. To the Jews. He had to get inside. He had a holy mission to carry out. He could save lives.

But Nikodem hadn't known what to do next. There was no safe way to enter the ghetto. How far was he going to stick his neck out for this mysterious Jew? So he kept the Jew in the cellar for months, feeding him potatoes and cabbage, waiting for a sign. But now time was running out; he had to figure out what to do with the stranger. He couldn't keep him down there indefinitely, especially with a few more months of winter remaining. Worse yet, the Kaczmareks had started prowling around the church, inspecting the belfries and peering through the stained-glass windows. Once one of them had even entered the church, striking terror into old Nikodem's heart. The man had stridden down the aisles as if he owned the place, stopping in front of the altar and glaring for a long time down at the rug. The bell ringer stood behind him, holding his breath, his eyes fixed on the wooden crucifix. Kaczmarek bent to the floor and ran his hand over the rug.

"What's this rug you got here, old Nikodem? It's old and worn like, like a Jewish prayer shawl! Ha, ha! Not exactly the kind of thing that belongs in a church, huh?" He spoke in a cold voice without raising his eyes from the ground.

✦

After the encounter with Kaczmarek in the church, the old man realized he had to warn Antoni. Nikodem had been waiting impatiently for his peasant friend for a few weeks, ever since the potatoes and cabbage had begun to run out. A number of German cars had recently been seen patrolling the road by the Kaczmarek Inn. They circulated around the Łagiewniki Forest before heading northeast toward Warsaw. Fugitives had been spotted as they traversed the snowy paths in the forest under cover of night. These were Poles who'd escaped German labor camps and were trying to cut through the Łagiewniki pine groves to reach the woods outside Parczew and Janów. They avoided the towns and villages, instead crossing open fields, meadows, and snow-covered forests on moonless nights. One of these men knocked on the door of the church late one night, hoping to change his soaked rags. Once he'd dried off, he agreed to convey a message from Nikodem to Antoni.

So now the two old friends sat together on a narrow bed that took up almost the whole room. It was more like an attic than an actual room. Many old Polish churches had such alcoves, with roofs joined at sharp angles like the wedge of a plough. In place of one of the walls, a slanted window filtered the dim light of the snowfields. Near them stood the little table where the severed hand of Saint Francis lay beneath its shroud. An oil lamp sent a dark haze up to the ceiling. As the men exchanged whispers, Antoni stared out the window toward the silent fields, where his horse had settled into a deep sleep.

Nikodem and Antoni had been friends a long time, going back to childhood. They shared memories of the frozen fields of Tannenberg in the First World War. They also discovered their families had been connected for generations; their great-uncles and cousins fought together in the tragic Polish insurrections of 1831 and 1863. Nikodem had searched feverishly through the old chronicles and yellowing registers that languished in the cellars of municipal buildings. The more he dug, the more threads he uncovered in the grand tapestry that linked past generations to him and his son, Tadeusz. He told Antoni of every detail, every new date, every obscure trace that proved their connection with long-deceased great-uncles. Left to himself, Antoni would have never contemplated such matters; he was content to spend his days on the dry land of the present day. Still he welcomed the bell ringer's discoveries, which brought them together under a warm glow of fellowship that insulated them now during the war's cruelest winter. Although their homes were miles apart, they visited each other regularly, sharing stories of long-dead relatives. Even now the two friends still dreamed of a glorious future for their country.

Ever since Antoni's son had also disappeared, he had lived in a constant state of worry. The Germans had threatened to cut off his head if his son did not return to their service; but, although nothing had come of this, the peasant did not feel safe. Now, as he sat on the edge of the bed, he was listening with rapt attention to Nikodem's hushed account. Antoni tugged at his thick mustache, which was beginning to thaw out in the heat of the room. When the bell ringer mentioned the stranger hiding in the cellar, Antoni dropped his hands into his lap, seized with fear. From outside they heard the jingle of the bells rocking in the night wind.

"This is really dangerous, Nikodem. Really dangerous," the peasant whispered after a long silence. "Of course we gotta do something. We gotta do something for him, but what? What *can* we do?"

"Every man must do what he can, what his heart tells him to do. Of course it's difficult. That's what war is all about, Antoni."

The peasant anxiously smoothed his mustache, which kept popping up again.

"D'you realize, Nikodem," he asked in a barely audible whisper, "what they're gonna do to you for hiding a . . ."

The bell ringer waved his hand in the air.

"I know, I know. At seventy years of age, Antoni, you see things a little differently. At seventy you can brush things off easier, everything except your *conscience*. And I ask you, what is the duty of a patriot? What is the duty of a true Pole? Do you understand me? Look at this little oil lamp." Nikodem pointed.

Antoni looked to the corner of the room where smoke was rising to the ceiling.

"Yeah, I see it. It'll go out soon."

"But what if we add a little oil. What then? It'll get brighter, right? I, and you, and thousands of others, we have to make sure the light doesn't go out, don't we? If it goes out, the whole world will be lost in darkness."

"Easy for you to say, my friend. It's natural to want to help your fellow man, but something always stops you, something gets in your way. Your hands are tied, see? A devil grabs you and shouts, 'No! Save your own life! That one's only a Gypsy, that one's a Turk, that one's a Jew.' I know we were all made by the same God, but we've got wolves all around us, I'm tellin' you, hungry wolves on all sides. Our people are no better than anybody else. Plenty of Poles have helped Hitler. That's our problem, Nikodem."

"That may be true, Antoni, but not everyone has become a wolf. There are still many like you and me in every town. But people refuse to speak up. They simply refuse—they're like mice hiding in a barn. That's what we're living in—an era of mice! Everyone is gnawing on their own shred of potato, biting their own fists. All this waiting around is a terrible sickness. I feel it myself! But believe me, Antoni, there are many who don't want to wait. They're getting impatient. Something's going to happen. After four years of war, they're still trying to keep the flame alive. And as for me? I'm going to be around long enough to strike my bells for victory. For a new homeland, a new Poland. Poland is not yet lost. 'Jeszcze Polska . . .'"

"But first, Nikodem, you're gonna strike your bells for the funerals of all the Jews in our country. Am I wrong?"

The bell ringer lowered his head to his chest. Both remained silent for a long time. As the room darkened, flame-colored shadows climbed the walls, cast by the oil lamp. The shadows rose, and the burning wick flickered, as if in fear. Moving to the window, the bell ringer stared at the world outside. The thoughts of both men turned to the stranger in the cellar. Nikodem had never seen him in broad daylight, but his dark silhouette now seemed to float about the room. It was as if the Jew were hovering over their heads like a bird beating its wings in terror. The bell ringer suddenly turned away from the window.

"At least our sons got away, Antoni. They don't have to stand around here with their hands tied. But *they* can't sleep either. People are getting stirred up."

"Who? The Jews?"

"Yes, he said they staged a rebellion, a real rebellion. In the Warsaw ghetto."

"The Jews? A rebellion? But they're so scared of death. They run away from a drop of blood."

"They're not the same Jews, Antoni. They're different. And their children are different. They're hardened, like ours. They're not afraid of death. Hitler has taught them a few things. These past years have been the toughest—they've been completely crushed. But they won't be able to do anything without help. Everywhere they're waiting for us, in every ghetto, every camp, waiting for our help.

And what are we doing, Antoni? What am I doing? And you? And thousands of others like us? What are we waiting for?"

Antoni suddenly remembered the vision that haunted him on the road through the forest: the Jewish family he'd once brought to the ghetto. He again felt the warm kiss of Moszek, the old Jew.

"And what's gonna happen to them, over there?" He thrust his hand over his mouth, as if trying to wipe away the Jew's kiss.

"Their cemetery keeps getting bigger and bigger; you can't even fit a dog into it anymore."

"And *him*—you're saying he wants to go in there?"

"We have to help him, Antoni. He's on some kind of mission—we have to help him."

Antoni nodded as he picked up a few twigs and tossed them onto the fire. The bell ringer stuffed shredded tobacco leaves into an old pipe. Looking around the storage room, Antoni suddenly understood why Nikodem needed so many potatoes and cabbages. There was no telling how long the stranger would stay down in the cold.

It was already long past midnight. A blue glow lit up the snow outside. Antoni gave up on the idea of going home. It was too late, and he was enjoying this chance to talk with his old friend, even under these circumstances. As they prepared for the night, the bell ringer pulled out a burlap sack from under the bed and laid it out near the stove. Then, as always before bed, the bell ringer went into the courtyard, this time accompanied by Antoni. They stood together on the blue-tinged snow, beneath the distant glow of the Milky Way. A bitter wind swept through the empty fields. They looked toward the horizon, where the pale orange beam of a searchlight swept over the ghetto. Nikodem squeezed Antoni's arm.

"Can you hear that, Antoni? Listen. Can you hear it? Someone's crying. It's a human voice. Listen! Listen! Someone's crying!"

"That's just the wind blowing in the woods, Nikodem. It's the wind, d'you hear? In the woods. Calm down! It's just the wind."

"The wind, you say? Listen. That's not the wind. Can't you hear it? That's a human voice. Someone's crying."

"No, Nikodem. I hear it now. That's the German dogs howling. Near the ghetto. The wind's carrying the sound."

Nikodem dragged Antoni out of the courtyard into the snowy field, lighting the way with a flashlight. They walked onward until they came upon a wooden cross set into a mound of snow. Antoni was seized with terror. At the foot of the cross were two bouquets of frozen flowers and a bunch of faded willow leaves.

The bell ringer dropped to his knees, removed his hat, and crossed himself.

"You see this?" He looked up at Antoni with tears in his eyes. "There were two people fleeing the ghetto, a brother and a sister maybe, still practically kids. It was dawn, and they started shooting at them. Then the poor kids fell, and the whole time the girl was yelling, 'Don't worry, they didn't get me, they didn't get me.' They fell right here, next to the bell tower, poor, poor children."

Antoni dropped to his knees as well.

"This is my evening prayer to you, Heavenly Son. Let them return, all the persecuted and betrayed. Let them return, all the Jews. Let them lie down among their own people and be alongside those they lived with. Our cross did not protect them while they were alive; may it at least protect them now, those poor wandering souls. Protect their bones, oh God, for the sake of the living who remain. Protect all our sons who are fighting the Devil."

A little while later, Nikodem delivered a dish of food into the cellar, and the two old men prepared for the night.

The bell ringer drifted off to sleep at once, but Antoni could not stop staring at the window. A cruel white light came into the room, surrounding him as he lay on his straw sack. Now he could plainly hear the wailing voice. Or was he only imagining it? Maybe it was the voice of the girl beneath the mound of snow. He fell into a deep sleep and dreamed of two children holding hands, running toward the church tower. He wanted to call out to them, run to them. He screamed out loud and woke with a start. In the glow of the night frost, he could make out the silhouette of Nikodem, sitting at the edge of his bed. Antoni watched as the bell ringer rose, moved toward the table, and uncovered the severed hand of Saint Francis. The fingers of the hand were pointed toward the window. Outside, the night was turning to a gray dawn—colossal snow-filled clouds floated by overhead like ghost ships over the Łagiewniki woods.

9

In the Cellar

The cellar was a long and narrow corridor, filled with empty barrels stacked to the ceiling, torn mattresses, broken bed frames, old clothes, dishes, and pots. All were from Jewish homes—all were covered in cobwebs. The barrels still gave off the dank stench of sauerkraut, harsh enough to make the eyes water. Pipes ran along the damp brick walls, but the bubbling song of the groundwater had not sounded inside them for a long time. The pipes hung like dark, bloodless veins. The cellar lay deep in the earth—it could only be accessed through a hole in the wall that led to a courtyard. As Vigdor climbed through the small opening, he felt as if he were slipping into a narrow grave.

The frozen darkness was illumined by an orange glow. Two candles rested against the pipes, lit with uncertain, trembling flames. Vigdor stretched his arms before him like a blind man. At first, he couldn't make out any of the faces around him. Then he became aware of the dark outlines of several men, wrapped in rags that almost completely covered their bodies. A sudden vision flashed before him: these veiled men were the Marranos of the ghetto! Outside in the streets, they bore a chastened, fearful look, but here in this dank cave they moved with strength and courage. Maybe their ancestors, resurrected after centuries of sleep, were now staring out of their eyes. As he stepped into the underground cellar, Vigdor felt like he had departed a realm of death and returned to the land of the living, where prayers ascended into the heavens like sprouting seeds yearning for the light.

A slender form approached Vigdor and placed an emaciated hand on his shoulder. Vigdor felt a shudder of shame as the man stammered a few sounds: "Vidaver. Chaim Vidaver."

Vigdor let himself be led onward, grasping the shaking bony fingers of the unfamiliar man. In the light of the candle, Vigdor glimpsed the man's bald head, which was wrinkled like old parchment. Chaim Vidaver's pale blue eyes shone with a look of kindness.

Gradually Vigdor realized that these were the people he had seen in Zelda's room. He recognized the man who had played the violin as Zelda lay dying. Vigdor was led into a dark corner, where another man was smoking a cigarette, the tip shining like a red eye in the darkness.

"Fellow Jews!" It was Chaim Vidaver intoning in a low voice. "Comrades! A new member has joined us today. From now on he will be one of us, bound to us in our secret, holy task. Like the rest of us. He comes to us through his connection to Zelda. Enough said. Welcome, Comrade Vigdor!"

The weak flames from the candles continued to flicker, and Vigdor sat down on the floor. He felt a hand slip into his. It was Gitele. Her small, unmistakable palm was warm to the touch.

Again, Vidaver's voice sounded in the darkness.

"Comrades, we must be very careful in everything we do. Only yesterday a terrible disaster nearly occurred just as we were relaying the news from the radio. You all know what it means to live in the ghetto. We are isolated; we've been completely abandoned by the outside world. We live in an ocean of death, surrounded by enemies. We have no idea what's happening half a kilometer away. Now, at the beginning of February, in the fourth year of our imprisonment, we are just as isolated as we were at the very start of the war. It's clear that we and we alone are responsible for our fate. What do we have to show for ourselves? Nothing but hunger and fear. Unless we are saved by some kind of miracle, annihilation awaits us. But where is this miracle? Where will it come from, I ask you? Are we strong enough to save ourselves? Or will we disappear like shadows in the night, without anyone knowing what became of us? We have only one choice: not to give in. Comrades, even though we've already endured so many years of disappointment and torment, things could change any day. Comrades! There are rumors about new transports—we could be the last to go. There are only seventy thousand of us left. Is there nothing we can do, I ask you? Will we hand ourselves over to the Germans for a loaf of bread, a little sugar and jam? Nobody knows where these transports are headed. Where are they taking our people? Where?"

A high-pitched voice interrupted Vidaver's speech.

"The last shipment of clothes they brought into the ghetto was stained with blood. Is that not enough for you, Comrade Vidaver?"

"For us here in this room, it *is* enough—we know what's going on. But everyone else in the ghetto, they don't want to believe it. Even after all they've seen, they can't believe such evil really is possible. And they're right: it's unbelievable. But what about us? What are we doing about it, we who know the truth? Future generations will never forgive us. Have we done *everything* that human beings ought to do? They won't believe us, our helplessness, our isolation. What we've been enduring in our era has never occurred in the history of our people. Has anything prepared us for this hell? Has *anyone* in the whole history of mankind had to face this? Are our souls and bodies up to the challenge? Our life is coming to an end—we are the last Jews. Who will reach out a hand to us? Where is the Almighty Creator? Where is our eternal God?"

Everyone was silent. Tears of wax spilled out from the candles, dripping onto the hollow pipes. Black smoke floated like a cloud over the ceiling. Outside, the night wind was rising in the north, sending vortexes of snow over the empty lots of the ghetto. It was as if an unseen, evil hand had stirred up the wind outside and was now forcing it through the cellar walls.

"But still we have our faith and hope," a second voice spoke up, soft and sincere as a child's. "Brothers, we still have one real hope: this little box. As long as we can hear voices from the outside, we're not cut off from the world. Even if the world refuses to listen to us. No one sees us behind these walls. But maybe, finally, someone will come and tell us what to do, where to look for help. Is it possible we've been completely forgotten? I can't believe it, my brothers. Maybe someone's already on the way, someone with good news. We can't simply die without receiving any signal from outside. Has the whole world been destroyed in this Flood? Are we the last Jews in a dead world?"

"We aren't the last ones, Comrade Vinkler," someone answered from behind a mountain of old mattresses. "Not the last. Our people have endured much and they'll outlive this hell. But what will they *know* about us? Nothing at all! Our own people have abandoned us, just like every other people on this earth! We must have committed some terrible sin against God, against our people, against the whole world. Even death can't erase such a sin."

Bitter laughter rang out in the cellar, as though an evil demon had been released.

"Ha, ha, ha . . ." The frightful voice rolled from one end of the cellar to the other—at first no one could tell if it belonged to a living being.

"Who dares mention death and sin? Are the Germans really the hand of God, sent to punish us? Has God designated the Germans to destroy His Chosen People? Ha! This is the sort of insane talk that comes from despair. We are nothing but stalks of wheat in a murderous world. And so it has always been. All around us, false messiahs bring blood and destruction. In their hearts, people are no longer holy. And we Jews? We're just an unhappy people in this unhappy family of nations on the earth."

"And the Germans? Are they also part of the human family?"

"The Germans themselves are stalks of wheat blown by the winds. It's true that we Jews are the weakest, the most often crushed. But remember that hate doesn't come from God, it comes from this world, from human beings. And people need to improve themselves here, in this short life that we have."

"But what about the divine mission of our people?" Chaim Vidaver spoke once again, his voice trembling with emotion. "What about everything we've given the world? What about our prophets? Our faith? Our God?"

"Our mission?" The sarcastic, devilish voice interrupted Vidaver. "Maybe our worthy Judenrat leader, Mordechai Chaim, that betrayer, that executioner—maybe he has also been selected by God? Ha, ha!"

"He's in the same boat as we are." A weak, hoarse voice rose from beside the burning candles. "Nobody knows how fate decides between people, how our lots are cast. Chaim must have good reasons for what he's doing. More than once I've seen him weeping as Jews were carted off, or on his way back from the city after meeting with the Germans, tearing his white hair out and sobbing."

"Those are the tears of a jackal, a madman's charade. He's sending the ghetto to its death. Does any man have the right to decide who will die? If everyone can't be saved, how can we save just a few, how can we decide someone's fate? What will future generations say? They'll say a handful saved themselves and sent the old, the weak, and the children to die. Is this the *sound reasoning* of the Jew who runs the ghetto? Shouldn't we all go to our death together—if everyone can't be saved? In a time of crisis, it's more honorable to accept death with courage than to live an unworthy life. A day will come, after this devastation, when only those who've died will look like pure Jews. People will look with suspicion into the eyes of every survivor, even those who seem the purest and most innocent."

"And if we're still alive now, if fate has protected us so far, does that mean we're all tainted? Haven't all of us been spared death by the good hand of fate?"

"Fellow Jews," an old man added his rough voice to the debate. "We *are* being killed for our sins—and for the sins of our fathers. This is what I firmly believe, comrades. But where is our savior?"

"What about the little babies who've died in the ghetto—what sins did they commit?" The satanic laughter rose again from the corner, bursting forth from the darkness and echoing like a doleful bell.

"Saviors. Faith. The one and only God, the God of the Chosen People. It's all a silly joke. Ha! Leave God alone in His heaven. Let Him sit on His throne and rule the stars for all eternity. He turned away from his Chosen People long ago. For all His great kindness, we've seen only darkness and cruelty. Our world isn't the kingdom of God but of godlessness. And still He remains silent. My only god is humanity, everything within creation. The ants, the wind, blood, a crust of bread, words between living human beings. All this is sacred. Only the world here below is sacred. Heaven is far, far away. I call this a place of ungodliness."

These heated exchanges in the dimly lit cellar brought strange relief to Vigdor's desolate heart. So many of the thoughts, questions, doubts, and accusations crisscrossing the room had tormented him for a long time. Until now, he'd been alone, like a flimsy, isolated vessel in a raging sea. Now that Gitele had brought him among these others, he felt a great consolation, even though the voices sounded desperate, angry, and shrill. Finally, he was hearing echoes of his own private confusions—about God, his fellow man, about life and happiness. These were *his* thoughts, *his* unexpressed doubts. He felt as though he had only just now been locked up in the ghetto, stripped of everything—but this time armed with strength to endure his people's unimaginable trials. His physical intimacy with Gitele after Zelda's burial suddenly came back to him; it stood before his mind's eye as a moment of weakness, a mark of shame threatening to darken the burgeoning hope he felt as he listened to the words in the cellar. He loosened his grip on Gitele's hand, which suddenly felt heavy and cold. Then he had a flash of insight into the workings of fate: eternal danger hung over the heads of all beings, but there was joy in solidarity with others, and *this* would have to suffice in the fight against evil. It was clear to him that even now, though the most bitter failures loomed for this tiny group, and their hopes would surely shatter like shards of glass, even now their dreams *were* coming true—the deep desire to escape the isolation of ghetto life and to regain a taste of the freedom that had been stolen from them. Dreams of liberty encircled the shadowy group like a cord of light. Vigdor felt protected by this light, and he was sure others did as well. He embraced Gitele and again felt the warm thrill of her narrow hips. Perhaps the very same spirit of God that hovered over the waters of the deep at the beginning of time was now carrying them onward over the primordial abyss.

Stirred by these emotions, Vigdor arose and spoke out, feeling slightly embarrassed though his form could barely be made out in the darkness.

"Brothers . . ." His voice wavered. "Our misfortune is so great. Nowhere in this vast world is there a place for us to hide. Even if somebody managed to escape the ghetto, they would be caught immediately. The villains serving the Germans are lurking everywhere. We have no underground tunnels, no forest. They've got us surrounded. There are no friends of the Jews for miles. It's just ourselves, ourselves and our courage."

But at that moment Chaim Vidaver hushed the room with a drawn-out *shh!* A crackling sound could be heard in the corner. The flickering flames on the tips of the candles were becoming smaller and smaller, but a much greater light shone through the black box on which Vidaver rested his hand. Now a human voice could be distinctly heard through the static. At first it hesitated, as if unsure of itself; then it burst forth, clear and bright, like lightning piercing the darkness of a stormy night. The voice was distant, as though from the infinite reaches of heaven, and yet close enough to touch everyone in their hearts. The assembled group leaned toward the corner to hear. It was a free voice, a woman's voice, reverberating with all the hope and purpose that human speech can attain. It began with sadness for a vanished world and moved on to rage for all the deaths wrought by a demon, sprung from hell. Then, finally, it vibrated with pity for all whom fate had designated as a sacrifice for the sake of a new world struggling to be born.

"All of you are victimized people. You don't know what fate awaits you. But don't think for a minute that the world will not punish the executioners. The day is near when accounts will be settled! Revenge will be exacted for all of the persecuted peoples. The undoing of that murderous nation has already begun: Stalingrad was the first fatal blow. Now the enemy will attack the weakest. After the Jews, it will be the Poles, and then others will follow. But ultimately they can't succeed. We must rise up! Jews in the ghettos! Poles in the prison camps! Save yourselves! Get an ax, a knife, an iron bar! Barricade your homes! Only by fighting do you stand a chance of survival! Fight! Help is on the way! The Warsaw Ghetto has been razed to the ground! Death to the enemy! Fight for your lives! Victory to the heroes of Treblinka, Auschwitz, Ponar, Sobibór! Victory is near! Victory for those who still hold God and mercy in their hearts! Mercy for all who suffer on this miserable earth!"

10

Black Birds

Franz Otto Jessicke could not understand why he felt like his chest was being squeezed in a vise. The pain darted from place to place, sometimes to the left, sometimes the right, sometimes dancing around his heart like a bubble in a carpenter's level. And what was worse, Obersturmbannführer Jessicke was now suffering from a furious headache that made his drooping eyelids look even heavier than usual. It gave him the dazed appearance of a chronic insomniac, though actually he'd recently been sleeping far longer than he should. Maybe this accounted for the deep lethargy in his bones and in his beer-filled belly. Otherwise, he could hardly explain the sudden, overpowering fatigue of someone whose sole responsibility was to man the guard post on the north side of the ghetto.

He wanted to leave this damned assignment and get as far away as possible. Why not volunteer for the Eastern Front, my dear Franz Otto? Stalingrad doesn't have to mean the end of all battles. In the meantime, those damned Russians are hiding out somewhere on the other side of the Dnieper. By the time they reach the Vistula River, we'll have our reinforcements. And the Bolshevik plague? Another Jewish plot, for sure. There's no other explanation. And what about the officers who went off to the Western Front? They'll all be taken prisoner, no question. Maybe it's all his doing, the all-powerful Jew-loving president from America, that damned Roos . . . Roos . . . Roosenvelt! Yes, there were so many things Franz Otto Jessicke would say if he could. Roosenvelt thought just like a Jew, that was for sure. But you just wait, my dear Juden-cripple, in this war every Jew will find himself one head shorter, get it?

Commander Franz Otto Jessicke had recently started talking to himself. Sitting in his desolate guard post, he would stare into the mirror hanging crookedly on the wall. He made faces at himself, twisting his swollen jowls, narrowing his eyelids, and then opening his eyes wide and raising his arm in a salute, standing at attention as if at a rally. All of this went back, he knew, to his early childhood when he was just a little *Schnauzebub* and he'd first fallen in love with the theater. His passion for acting had lain dormant for many years, but now, sitting at his post, it was coming back to him. He grinned at himself as he listened to his own wonderful line delivery. Then he burst into uncontrollable laughter, which roared through his massive body like beer rushing through a crack in a barrel. He reached down and grabbed the sagging folds of his belly to hold the laughter in.

"In this war every Jew will find himself one head shorter, get it?"

Just then Jessicke felt a twinge of pain in his belly.

He grabbed his mug of beer and swished it around until a thick white foam slid over the rim and dampened his fingers. Then, he downed the swirling liquid, his tongue sliding over his yellowing buckteeth. All the while, he scanned the outside world with a look of suspicion and concern.

As the winter evening deepened, a thick mist settled over the fields and the guardhouse. Frosty air rushed through the open window. Still, the room was suffused with a dry, stifling heat. It came from the stove where twigs and branches from the surrounding forest were burning. Jessicke was parched. Thank God the Polish inn was still here in this Jewish hellhole. On the floor under the bed stood a square crate, filled with empty bottles. Jessicke sat by the open window, staring into the fields. The sun hung low in the sky, as if stalled on its way down. Pink streaks ran across the sky over the western side of the ghetto.

So many months had gone by exactly like this, sitting in front of the window, observing the guards pacing by the ghetto wall. Until now, it had never occurred to Commander Jessicke to focus his gaze so strongly on the sun. Its red-orange crown was probably suspended at this very moment over the Rhine. Soon it would pass Thuringia and then descend slowly over Hamburg before vanishing into the sea. "Yeah, those big shots in Berlin are completely nuts," he muttered to himself. "God help us! First it was: Do whatever you can with these Jewish turds! We'll give you free rein. Total freedom! So we did what we wanted, and a fine job we did, too. A man isn't like a rabbit or a bird. Animals don't have eyes like *theirs*. Like those damned Jew-eyes. Back at home yours truly was the best hunter, the quickest shot. Ach, those Sundays in the Thuringian Forest. God, just think of it! What fun we had in the days of the evictions! Just when the ghetto was being set up. You could stand by a window just like this and aim at all the Jews walking past the barbed-wire fences. From far off they looked just like little rabbits. Ha! No, not like rabbits. Like wild hens, like big, plump wild hens. Or maybe black birds. But for the last few months: 'Shooting strictly forbidden . . . *verboten*.' I'm sorry, but this is nuts! If not for the Jews, there'd be no point to this war at all. They make the whole thing easier to bear, isn't that right? So how come the fancy people in Berlin decided to stop us having our little fun? God only knows! It's all politics. The front—death; retreat—death. It's a good thing we get a raven flying by once in a while, the black spirit of the ghetto Jews. And then: *bang!* God have mercy. No, no, no. Those guys in Berlin are all crazy, totally crazy. *Verstanden?* You understand?"

Sitting by the window overlooking the northern fields of the ghetto, Franz Otto Jessicke sunk deeper into his thoughts. The only way to deal with this monotony and the pain gnawing at his chest like a mouse buried inside him was to think back to the single undying pleasure from his youth: shooting. It wasn't so much the gratification of aiming and hitting something, but the sheer joy of pulling the trigger: the sudden explosion, the rush of air, the deafening silence after the *bang*. It all had something grand and solemn about it, as if he, Franz Otto Jessicke, with his own two hands could unleash the ferocious, destructive power of nature. And so, as soon as he'd dispatched the guards to patrol the fences around the ghetto, he would take out his black shotgun and gaze out toward the horizon. And then every passing bird became a poor cripple, hobbling over the fields with a broken wing, or else collapsing in the snow.

What amused him most were the crows who got away with only a wounded wing. First they were just black spots in the air; then they fell zigzagging into the snow, and you could hear the *caw, caw, caw* of a wounded crow calling for help. Sometimes they stood up and tried to fly with their one good wing. But after a few hops they usually sunk down into the snow, crying out over the fields. And then something strange would happen: As soon as a bird cried out in distress, the sky would darken with a black cloud of birds flying in from the nearby woods. They would circle over the wounded bird. It was then that Franz Otto Jessicke would give in completely to his desires: Some ten birds would come falling out of the sky, almost all at once. He could hit every one. Don't bother offering any help or even showing mercy, you damn Jewish birds! *Jawohl!* No pity! War is war. *Verstanden?*

The more Jessicke shot the birds, the more they avoided the fields beyond the ghetto walls. Sometimes he heard them cawing deep in the Łagiewniki Forest. They were hiding out, holding their secret gatherings high in the pine trees. Conspiratorial cackles echoed through the air like the muffled voices of men and women shut up in coffins. Even so, although fewer and fewer birds were flying past the ghetto, Franz Otto Jessicke was working out new ways to practice his marksmanship.

Not far from the guardhouse there stood an old, dying tree, its bare, black branches clinging to the ancient trunk. It stood alone among the snowdrifts, rooted deeply in the earth. Now that the Germans had destroyed the surrounding houses, it seemed even more solitary than before. From a distance, it looked like an immense ghost returned to the world after long centuries of sleep. Its crooked trunk was covered with dark green moss and its branches were so thick that they blocked the snow from the ground, leaving a perennially damp, bare patch around its base. In earlier days, when he was permitted to open fire directly on the ghetto, Franz Otto Jessicke had hardly noticed the tree at all. It was only later, once the birds had become scarce, that the tree came into focus. Now it stood out firm and unmovable like a dark, otherworldly giant refusing to abandon a child's gravesite. Armed with his black rifle, Franz Otto engaged the old tree in heated battle, firing round after round.

As the pointed bullets pummeled the massive trunk, desiccated chunks of bark peeled away and fell to the ground. The branches cracked and hung limp like the arms of wounded men. Still the bare heart of the tree stood unmoved, its ancient roots digging into the soil. And so the battle between Commander Jessicke and the dying tree raged on, neither side willing to surrender. When the German's bullets rained down like hail for hours at a time, the tree seemed to grow even more defiant. Eventually Jessicke tired of this game, and that was when he left the window and stood before the mirror, spending hours saluting his own reflection.

✦

Commander Franz Otto Jessicke probably would have ended it all if he hadn't received new orders from Berlin. Finally! He was getting so sick of sitting around this damned Jewish quarter. A man must *do* something—either with his hands or with his mind. *Nicht wahr?* The orders from Berlin roused him from his stupor. He felt the blood flowing through his veins again. Even the pinched feeling in his chest began to fade away. The secret orders handed down from Berlin were very simple: go after all the illegal partisans wherever the German fist was in control. The partisans had become a plague all over occupied Poland—and not only in the forests and villages. In fact, the orders mentioned no particular place, only that the partisans had to be weeded out. It *was* made very clear that anyone not German might be a secret partisan. All non-Germans were enemies—except, of course, the proven allies who fought side by side with German sons. After the great victory, they too would reign over the world for a thousand years. The order also included a special note:

> Above all, we must keep a close eye on the Jewish settlements. All surveillance systems must be strengthened. Numerous incidents have already occurred in which members of the secret Jewish brotherhood have escaped the ghettos and joined the illegal resistance in the forests. Orders have therefore been given to all commanders to destroy immediately all inhabited and

> uninhabited buildings along the periphery of the ghetto. The inhabitants of these buildings serve as liaisons connecting the illegal partisans with Jews in the ghetto. They serve the enemy apparatus in their fight against the German people. All SS commanders are hereby obligated to fulfill this order. Heil Hitler!

What a joy to receive this secret order from Berlin. Finally! He marched across the floor, goose-stepping as if in formation. Twice he paused in front of the mirror; he stuck out his breast, gazing at the glistening bronze medal of honor. He saluted to himself and bellowed in his low voice, "*Deutschland, Deutsch-land, üb-er all-es.*" Then he pulled out his pen, and, in his best Gothic script, he began writing the first of two advisory notices. The first was for the Pole who owned the Kaczmarek Inn. And the second—the second . . . the second? Heh, heh, heh, heh!

At this thought Commander Jessicke burst into such resounding laughter that the empty beer bottles under his bed began to rattle. His belly jiggled so violently that he had to reach down and hold it in place.

The commander knew the inn wouldn't be an easy nut to crack. Kaczmarek had a long arm—it might reach as far as the regional commander himself. Kaczmarek often traveled to Poznań on business, though never alone, that Polish swine. Ha, ha! His pretty younger sister might come in handy, that little Polish hen. Come here, you little, Kacz . . . Kacz . . . Kaczmarek! God have mercy! But this time, Mr. Kaczmarek, it's an order and it comes from a trifle higher up than Poznań: it's from Berlin itself, my dear Kaczmarek. Let's see if that old dog will let me play with his sister! Well, well, we'll just see about that. In the meantime, we'll start with the building in the second order—we'll knock down that wooden ruin.

He wasn't sure whom to put in charge of knocking down the strange little black building in the fields, just east of the ghetto fence. He was surprised he hadn't taken care of it himself. Truth is, he'd never even looked inside to see what it was. A sudden fantasy set his blood aflame: What if that old pig Kaczmarek sent that little chick to pay him a night visit in *that* very building? Hee, hee. Wouldn't that be romantic? Not to mention far from those jealous officers.

He raised his puffy eyes and gazed out the open window at the deserted, snowy fields. Although the sun had set long ago, its weary, melancholy glare still reflected off the snow. A rose-colored haze wrapped around the black tree like a coat. Spots of sun dotted the dangling, dead branches, looking from far away like golden sparrows.

The commander saluted himself once again in the mirror. This time it was too dark to see his image. He wasn't sure what made him happier: the letter he'd received from Berlin or the image of the little Polish hen that suddenly appeared in his weary mind. He could see her so clearly, with her devilish smile, could feel her standing before him, naked in the darkness. He slowly opened a narrow closet door. It couldn't hurt, he whispered to himself, to bring over the golden bottle of French cognac. He gently shook the bottle in the dark and listened to the muffled sound of the liquid bubbling inside. But Franz Otto Jessicke imagined it was the back of her neck, and that he could hear a gentle whisper from her warm lips.

11

Purifying the Dead

No one understood why the Germans set up the ghetto with the graveyard inside, while leaving the small synagogue outside. A tall, rusty barbed-wire fence now surrounded the graveyard, which lay next to an open field where only weeds and tall potato shrubs grew. The red-brick synagogue was a squat building, divided into two sections, with narrow windows under the eaves. Over the years, the walls had taken on a grayish tint. They were crisscrossed by black streaks that looked like charred markings of fiery tongues. One entrance led to the prayer hall, the other to a small room where the dead were purified. Built long ago before the cholera epidemic, the synagogue had been witness to countless weddings and circumcisions. Once the new burial ground was set up and the room for purifying corpses was added, the synagogue had been constantly filled with the sounds of eulogies and lamentations.

All of this was long before the ghetto was formed. As soon as the Germans set foot on Polish soil, they took God's house from the Jews, along with their room for purifying the dead. After four years of war, the disgraced synagogue had become a ruin, sinking deeper and deeper into the dark soil. Its sloping roof still housed the panel showing the stone tablets, but the Hebrew letters had chipped off and lay abandoned near the ghetto fence. Inside the synagogue, the walls still bore the markings of Jewish prayers that someone had once engraved in the plaster. Dust covered the walls like a death shroud, and a faint glimmer of light shone through a window near the ceiling. Nobody had set foot inside the synagogue since the ghetto had been built. Members of the Landsturm regiment who patrolled the ghetto fence kept at least three meters' distance. They hardly dared peek through the windows, as if fearful that the mysterious power of the Jewish God was still present in the deteriorating building, waiting to burst forth in vengeance.

Just before leaving for the ghetto, local Jews nailed heavy boards across the front door to block access to the house of God. But the room in back, where burial rites were performed, was left unprotected, and the doors had long since been torn off. Peasants from nearby villages flocked into the abandoned room to break up the black marble floor with axes and haul off the tiles. A few broken shards were still lying in the corners. The ground beneath the floor was now exposed, and wispy grass shoots had sprung up. Sparrows had built a nest in the window; spiderwebs spanned the ceiling. The only sign of the room's former use was a wide, wooden board where the dead had been laid out when their last rites were performed.

Guards neglected the area behind the old synagogue because it lay on the northern side of the ghetto, where no living soul had been seen for a long time. The fields were overgrown with weeds and brambles. Strange flowers with heart-shaped petals occasionally sprang up. Sometimes, when Commander Jessicke was shooting at the birds, an injured crow would drag itself to the deserted building and seek refuge under the board that had been used for purifying the dead. It could take days for it to die. Meanwhile the guards along the ghetto fence would hear outlandish sounds from inside like the shrill cries of abandoned infants.

The commander had already sent his letter to the inn. Now he was eagerly expecting a visit from the Polish girl. His plan was to welcome her with a smile; then he would take her for a little walk to the strange room behind the synagogue.

✦

It was a bleak winter evening. Although no snow had fallen the entire day, a biting wind was blowing in from the north, sharp as a switchblade. It scattered diamond-like flakes of snow. At twilight, the wind settled down. A mild breeze stirred around the graveyard and floated in through the ghetto fence. The night watchmen had long since departed on their nightly rounds along the perimeter. Franz Otto Jessicke stood in front of the window at his post, wrapped in a fur coat, two bottles of cognac peeking out of his pockets. The commander was getting impatient. According to the deal he'd struck the day before at the Kaczmarek Inn, the girl should be there already. Through the deepening night fog, he could just barely make out the dancing orange lights of the inn. It was to be demolished in a matter of days. To be perfectly honest, it would be a loss for him and his comrades. Maybe he ought to write to Berlin, tell them to drag the thing out a little. Though the food they got from the army dispensary was nothing to complain about, it was good to a have a nice tavern around. As he stared into the darkness, he saw a shadow moving up the road past the inn. It hardly looked like a person. Covering himself with his fur coat, he wandered away from the guard post.

Night had fallen, and darkness swept over the fields like an immense whale swimming through the sky. A solitary shivering star was visible overhead. The commander walked along the snowy path leading to the sinister building. Thick brambles had sprung up alongside the condemned synagogue. He stood by the entrance near the back room. He turned, and once again surveying the road leading to the inn, he could see someone running toward him. It was her—the Polish girl. He opened his coat to catch her, and dragged her through the open door into the abandoned prayer room.

This was not his first fling in occupied Poland. But no other time had been anything like this. What was happening now was like crossing a whole new frontier. Right here, in this cursed Jewish temple? Ha! Ha! How delicious to look right in the face of the all-powerful, mysterious God of the Jews—and to scorn Him! To have *his* way! Ha! And that wasn't all. So many years he'd watched the innkeeper's sister and never done anything—and now she was falling into his lap like, like a helpless little bird. All this was too sudden, too thrilling for the commander. What was this? His heart was beating so hard, he thought he could hear it echoing under the medal of honor bouncing on his chest. How's that for Teutonic passion! A medal of honor for banging a girl in a Jew temple! Then he remembered he had to calm himself. He remembered what his Anne-Marie once said in the heat of passion; she said, "Oh, Otto, Otto, you have to watch out—one of these days, you're going to drop dead while you're making love." Well, there you have it: my old lady in Berlin with her crazy ideas, like all women. But why did her words come back to him right then, just as he was leading a sweet girl into the darkness of a strange, abandoned room? He pulled the cognac bottles from his pockets and set his coat down on the board where the Jews laid out their dead.

They sat together for a long time in the dark, taking swigs of the luxurious French libation. Then the girl was startled by something—she stood up and looked around. What was that hunched, white figure who'd just floated over the board? She whispered to the commander what she'd seen. Their nervous laughter echoed off the walls, filling the room with a dizzying sound. It was only the light of the moon, shining through the window bars, nothing more. Still, the girl couldn't calm down. She huddled against the commander's chest. Franz Otto had already had too much to drink. He had the funny feeling a menacing dwarf was racing around in his brain, lashing him with a whip. He pressed his mouth to the girl's moist lips, as his hands descended her soft neck.

It wasn't long before the commander collapsed on the board and fell asleep. He was suddenly so deeply asleep that he didn't even stir when the girl let out a cry and ran out into the night. Some time later, with his body still spread out over the board and his head resting on the wood, he opened his eyes, his lips forming barely audible words. Franz Otto must have been quite drunk. But why did he have that pinched feeling in his chest again? Maybe it was only the medal of honor pressing against him. He tore the medal from his chest and threw it across the room. It crashed against the wall and fell to the floor with a metallic clang. Then Anne-Marie's words rattled through his head once again: "One of these days." What if her mad prophecy should come true? What, then, Franz Otto? "One of these days. One of these days, you'll die." Her words grew softer and softer, and now she seemed to be sobbing. He fell asleep again, gurgling incomprehensible sounds.

And it was then that Franz Otto Jessicke, commander of the ghetto watch, splayed on the board in the abandoned synagogue just beyond the fence of the ghetto, had one final, incredible vision. Maybe it was a drunken delusion—or maybe the unadorned perception of absolute truth.

He heard them coming. First one by one, then two by two, then three by three, and finally in unbridled multitudes. Some flew down from the heights of heaven and others rose from the earth. At first it looked like a giant dark cloud, then an endless procession of black birds, circling around his head. Some landed on the ground and hopped toward him on one leg or dragging a broken wing. Then they circled his head, again and again. He could tell they were the Jew-birds he used to shoot down from the sky above the ghetto. Stronger birds were carrying wounded ones on their backs; dead birds were falling from the sky, staining the snow. Blood rushed around the ghetto gates like a river. Suddenly one of the birds peeled out of the sky and dove straight at him. Others followed and soon an entire flock was pecking at his chest. He tried to cry out, but no sound came from his mouth. The birds covered his body, and he couldn't lift a hand to drive them away. The moon gazed down through the clouds as the birds exacted their punishment.

Then suddenly they flew off, an immense black cloud rising to the sky. The beating of wings resounded through the air as they climbed toward the moon, which hung like a frozen orb over the fields of death. When the commander finally opened his eyes, he saw a circle of men standing around him holding candles. He scarcely recognized the faces. When he tried to prop himself up on his elbows, he collapsed onto the long board in one final, agonized spasm.

Much later, his fellow commanders carried his cold, exposed body back to the guardhouse. Their heads were bowed in respect. His body was so heavy it was like hauling away a marble statue. As the procession moved along the narrow, snow-covered path, the moon lit up his face, and they saw that it was twisted into a scream. Dark liquid dribbled from his mouth, forming a band like a black rope around his neck.

12

Piles of Clothes

Panic-stricken, Marta Kaczmarek fled the room behind the synagogue and raced through the fields. When she reached the inn, she found her brothers, Stefan and Adam, standing by the window, whispering to one another. A cool evening mist floated in from outside, and the hall smelled faintly of garlic and sour cabbage. All the guests had already gone home. The only light in the hall came from a lamp illuminating the golden frame around an image of the Blessed Virgin. In the brothers' hands was the letter from Commander Jessicke, ordering them to abandon the inn.

The two brothers were well aware that Marta had visited the commander earlier in the evening. They had anxiously awaited her return, but now they were arguing so intently that they hardly noticed Marta as she came through the doorway, out of breath. She watched them from the other side of a glass cabinet filled with beer bottles, empty jugs, and plates of leftover venison sausage. Through the cracked window leading to the kitchen, she could hear the hiss of damp wood burning in the fireplace. The brothers cut starkly different figures: Stefan's flaxen hair drooped over his face, while Adam's bald head was crossed by blue veins. Adam was clutching Stefan by the wrist as Stefan tried to free himself.

"No Kraut is going to kick a Kaczmarek off his land! It's still our land after all! This is our Poland!"

He ripped the paper up furiously, threw the pieces on the ground, and trampled them defiantly with his black boots.

Adam stared back at his older brother in terror. Stefan's anger was exploding like a flood bursting through a dam. His eyes narrowed into tiny slits, sharp as the edge of a scythe. Adam knew his brother was capable of great things, but could he avert the danger hanging over the Kaczmarek family? The edict of expulsion was the most barbaric act the Germans had committed since the war began. It had come out of the blue—and just when they stood to make a killing. Word had gone around that the Germans were laying down new tracks for a railway line heading westward from Marysin. It was supposed to pass right by their inn. And the brothers knew what that meant: business was about to be booming around here. No more quiet little life near the ghetto. And this was the moment the Germans picked to throw them out?

Stefan was so beside himself that he was almost unrecognizable. It had all started a few weeks earlier with his surprise trip to Saint Francis of Assisi, where he'd discovered the bell ringer's little secret. Ever since then Stefan kept going out to the doorstep in front of the inn to peer at the church belfry rising over the Łagiewniki woods. For hours, he would pace wordlessly around the inn, growing more and more agitated, like a hunting dog who'd caught the scent of wounded prey. Adam had no idea what was on his brother's mind. Stefan, meanwhile, knew he had to take advantage of his discovery, but he wasn't sure how. He knew this knowledge could gain him something valuable. He had only one fear: that something would happen overnight and his secret knowledge would be rendered useless. He reassured himself that the Jew wouldn't fly his cage so easily. He'd be too frightened to leave just yet. He'd hold on for a while in the dark cellar until he gathered his strength.

Still, it was foolish to wait—why should he? You never knew what tricks they might try. So he resolved to go see the Kraut the very next day and propose a trade. He'd tell him straight, "Look, I can offer you a rare bird, as long as you don't touch the inn." The German would definitely go for it. Who knew how rare the bird really was? Stefan was lucky the shooting had stopped so quickly. One day he'd returned to the chapel—to check up on Grandpa Załucki. He had no trouble hoisting himself up to the window, despite the icy ledge. Peering inside, he could clearly make out the bell ringer busying himself with something in front of the altar. Did his eyes deceive him? Damned scum, the dog was a sellout to the Jews! Is this how he honored their holy Saint Francis? And where? Right in front of the holy altar? At the feet of the Son of God! It was the infidel Jews who had nailed him to the cross to begin with!

Throughout these tense days, Stefan Kaczmarek often pondered everything that had befallen the Jews since the war began, how they'd been caught and stuck in ghettos, how they'd lost all the wealth they'd stolen from poor, helpless Poland over the course of centuries. He thought about all the beatings delivered to their curly, black-haired heads, heads that had conspired with Satan to hatch evil plots enslaving the farmers and laborers, noble Poles one and all. And when he lost himself in vague speculation about the Jews and how they had become the masters of Poland, he always reached the same conclusion: their downfall was none other than the hand of God punishing the wicked, the nonbelievers, the rebels who'd betrayed the Son of God. It was clearer to him now than ever before that the world was in the hands of merciful Jesus Christ, in the hands of the Church. The *Żydzi* had murdered the one and only God and now they had to pay for it. Vengeance was raining down from heaven above—and it would never cease for as long as Jewish vermin still stalked the earth.

Stefan saw himself as a proud knight united in struggle with thousands upon thousands, joined together in a secret order. Together they would usher in the reign of the crucified God. Stefan's own hands were instruments of God's vengeance. He knew the risk of losing resolve, so he tried to imbue everything he did in this ghetto wasteland with a special piety, linking him to all the others who bore the holy symbol of God in their hearts.

✦

When Marta stepped inside and started telling them what had happened to the commander, her brothers were stunned. Everything was thrown into confusion. Marta collapsed onto a wooden bench near the bar and let loose a stream of barely articulate words. The commander's fate would make people suspicious; her brothers might be implicated. Stefan couldn't tear his eyes away from his sister's tormented face, which was glowing like a red apple in the dim light of dusk.

"He's dead? Are you sure?" Stefan asked, making the sign of the cross over his heart.

"Yes, yes, I'm sure. It must have been some kind of stroke."

Stefan began to pace back and forth from the door to the kitchen. In the glow cast by the kerosene lamp, his cheekbones seemed to shake. His bloodless hands jerked up and down, hardly seeming to belong to his body.

The commander's death filled him with dread unlike any he had ever felt. He fixed his eyes on Marta as she nervously fiddled with the gold cross around her neck. Who knew what kind of devil might replace Commander Jessicke? They might be doomed—not even Stefan's discovery of the secret hiding place in the chapel would save them. Then he had a sudden flash of inspiration. He reached for a keychain hanging on the wall and headed for the kitchen. Outside, the wind had picked up, hurling whirlwinds of snow against the windows. Adam and Marta stared blankly as Stefan opened the door near the stove and climbed a narrow staircase up to the attic. He turned and beckoned for them to follow. As Marta and Adam climbed the stairs, the kerosene lamp in Marta's hand let off a ghostly light.

✦

Standing side by side in the corridor in the attic, Stefan, Marta, and Adam swept away the cobwebs covering a tiny door. Then came a metallic clanking; it was Stefan's key turning in the old lock. He squeezed into the dark attic room, followed by Adam and finally Marta, still carrying the kerosene lamp. They were greeted by the musty smell of old fabric, rotting suitcases, trunks, and satchels. There were countless handbags and stacks of wool jackets, multicolored shirts, and trousers. There were also piles of silk scarves, pelisses, fleece-lined handkerchiefs, and leather bags. All had once belonged to Jews. Bronze, copper, and silver dishes peeked out of half-opened chests. Broken-off dolls' legs sat on blue crystal plates next to flower vases. There were lidless teapots, silver Shabbos candlesticks, and Hanukkah menorahs. One side of the room was devoted to heavy mink, skunk, and astrakhan coats. Another had mostly women's clothes: satin and velvet dresses, bathrobes, and stockings. All of it flickered in the pale glow of Marta's kerosene lamp. A narrow skylight looked out on the Polish night, where the northern star shone between heavy snow clouds drifting with the wind.

Stefan feverishly inspected the piles of clothes. Now that Commander Jessicke was dead, along with their hopes of bargaining for a reprieve, it was foolish to keep these old belongings at the inn. Everything had to go at once. But to where? Best to send them to Uncle Michałek in Łęczyca. He could sell some of them on his journeys through the countryside. The Germans took all confiscated Jewish possessions to Poznań, sometimes as far as central Germany. It was madness to keep these things one more day at the Kaczmarek Inn.

Marta set the lamp on the floor and began sorting clothes alongside Adam and Stefan. They opened trunks, suitcases, and overflowing baskets, rummaging feverishly through moldy linen, damp pillows, clothes, kitchen utensils, and children's toys. With each transport of Jews into the ghetto or to unknown destinations in the East, these abandoned objects had steadily piled up. Now, as the Kaczmareks sifted through the Jews' former possessions, clouds of dust wafted into the air, so thick they seemed like the shades of their former owners. And now they all seemed to surface again, these Jews with suitcases on their hunched shoulders. They were carrying bags draped in old blankets with dangling cups and bowls. Good God! How many useless things they'd carried to the wagons waiting for them at the railyard beyond the cemetery. They'd marched onward, these Jews, their faces sunken toward the earth. What had they been looking for on the unresponsive ground, in the sand by the road, in the waving grass? The more Stefan, Adam, and Marta sifted through clothes and old objects, separating out the most valuable items, the more the attic filled with ghostly Jews, marching toward their awful fate. The Kaczmareks heard indistinct sounds overhead, noise like an approaching storm. They understood it was the crying of women and children who could no longer keep up with the throngs of the hunted.

After plowing through endless suitcases and old clothes, their hands finally touched the floor. There they discovered countless small velvet bags. Some bore strange inscriptions, embroidered with silver and gold thread. They had never seen this sort of writing, nor did they remember if they had searched through the bags before throwing them on the attic floor. The Kaczmareks hadn't had time to inspect all the valuables the Jews left behind. These velvet bags had been buried for years under a mountain of suitcases. It was only now, after clearing away so many things, that they could inspect these mysterious objects that the Jews had obviously treasured.

In the wavering light of Marta's lamp, Stefan picked up one of the bags and opened it. He pulled out two small black boxes, surrounded by narrow strips of dark leather. Adam handed him another bag, and Stefan removed its contents as well, and so on, until there was a mountain of black boxes on the floor in front of them. Stefan unrolled the leather strips, and little cubes fell to the floor. They looked at each other in wonder. So this is where the Jews hid their greatest treasures. This was a new bit of Jewish trickery.

Taking out his penknife, Stefan began cutting into one of the black cubes. The thin walls yielded easily to his blade, and out came a rolled-up parchment. It looked almost green in the light of the kerosene lamp. A mysterious glow came from the velvet covering the wall of the box. Stefan kept slicing into the boxes only to find more and more little scrolls, all alike. He unrolled one and slid his fingers over the parchment, which was cold as ice. Spread before him, it revealed strange Jewish letters. Some were pointed, others round; others leaned over as if about to fall. The slim black lines of text danced like butterflies in the flickering light of the lamp. As Stefan stared at his unfathomable discovery, the howling wind came seeping through cracks in the window frame. A silver ray of light shone into the attic from the pale moon, illuminating the silent figures bent over heaps of scrolls.

Marta hurried to her feet. The moonlight filled her with the same dread she had felt in the building in the fields near the ghetto. There, too, the moonlight had been an ominous sign. She crossed herself nervously and spoke aloud the names of all the saints she could recall. She begged her brothers to leave the attic, but they were preoccupied with the scattered pieces of white parchment.

"We have to get to Michałek. To Michałek," Stefan hissed between clenched teeth.

"To Łęczyca? You want to see Michałek?" Adam asked, straightening himself up from the floor.

Marta and Adam found the door and descended the staircase, leaving Stefan alone in the attic. The darkness below was illuminated by the lamp. Brother and sister waited anxiously at the bottom of the stairs. Finally, Stefan joined them, still clutching one of the velvet phylactery bags, leather straps hanging from the sides. He stuffed it in his back pocket, his face twisted into a grin. Outside the window, the winds became increasingly violent. The snow blew into a maelstrom of blinding whiteness.

13

The Tower

That very night, while the Kaczmareks were in their attic, sorting through piles of Jewish possessions, the old peasant Antoni was in the church, unable to sleep. Half awake, he saw the silhouette of a figure rising before him, a shadow floating across the room. Now it came to rest near the bell ringer's bed. Antoni shot up. Could it be real? He rubbed his eyes and stared again, but the shadow had vanished.

Antoni sat up in his straw bed, listening in the darkness. Snow began pelting the window of the chapel, and a furious wind pounded the roof, shaking the shingles. Meanwhile the bell ringer, Nikodem, kept snoring away, deep in sleep. All of a sudden he let out a wail and began waving his arms, as if struggling with someone in his dream. Antoni gently touched his raised hand, and the old man awoke, sat up, and wiped the sweat from his forehead.

"*Boże, Boże!* Oh God, oh God!" Nikodem whispered. "Is that you, Antoni?"

"Yes, it's me. What frightened you, old man?"

"I had a dream. A strange dream, Antoni."

"Do you remember it?"

"Oh, I remember. Such a strange dream! I had a vision. A very strange dream."

"So tell me," Antoni begged him. "I don't usually put much stock in dreams, but let's hear it."

"It's hard to describe. It was Christmastime. There was a large crowd downstairs in the church, people from every village, from the whole district. They were all kneeling and praying, and suddenly,

I can still see it, Saint Francis himself was standing there leading the Mass. He gestured with his hand, and then, Antoni—a miracle! The Son of God slowly descended from his great cross of wood, half naked. He walked past the kneeling crowd. With every step, he left a drop of blood on the floor. Saint Francis was supporting him as he led him to the pulpit. Nobody even looked up. Then, suddenly, the Son of God turned his face to me. I let out a cry. Oh, Antoni, this must be a sign from heaven!"

"I don't believe in signs from heaven, Nikodem. I'm just a simple farmer. You know I'm no heretic—I try to be a good man. I stand by the church like a true Catholic should. But I can't believe God sends His messages in dreams. Don't you think He would speak to you in the clear light of day so you could understand Him? That's what I think. Why would He speak to you in a dream?"

"You're talking like an unbeliever, Antoni. Even the Tatars believe in their dreams."

"I can't tell you what the Tatars believe," Antoni answered in a quiet voice. "All I know is whatever happens in a dream is sent by the Devil, you can bet. He's just toying with you. *Bóg wiara, sen mara . . .* It's Satan's game, pure and simple. Spit on the ground, Nikodem. Wake up. Our sons gave up superstitions long ago."

"Are you telling me, Antoni, that seeing the face of the Son of God is a superstition?"

"You're telling me you've really seen the face of the Holy Son? With your own eyes?"

"With my own eyes. I swear by all the saints. But listen, Antoni, that's not all. Oh, Lord, please forgive all my sinful thoughts and feeble human words. Do you know, Antoni, who else I saw? Do you know who Saint Francis was carrying?"

"You told me you saw the crucified Son of God."

"No, no, no. Antoni, it was *him*, the one living downstairs."

"Who?"

"The strange man. The Jew under the altar, down in the cellar."

"You see, then. Just what I said—it's all the work of the Devil. His little game."

"Yes, it was the strange man. No doubt about it. Just as he was when I last saw him. And I heard his voice too. The Saint of Assisi was holding him the whole time. He was leading him somewhere, toward the corner by the window, where it's always pitch-black. Then they both disappeared through the window, as if on a cloud. Oh God. *Boże, Boże!* Oh God."

"Nikodem, please. You've been snared by the Devil. That's what it is. Now, I ask you, when have you ever seen anybody get carried away on clouds?"

"Is it not written that Saint—I forget his name, but is it not written that he flew to heaven on a cloud? Listen to me, Antoni, this was a message sent directly from heaven. It can't be anything else." The bell ringer crossed himself several times and lowered his graying head all the way to the ground.

"A sign, you say? But of what?"

"That the time is right. The time is *now*. We have to let the strange man out of the cellar. Tomorrow might be too late. I'll show him the way to the ghetto fence, just over the field. God will lead him onward from there—and protect him."

"Nikodem, you really believe this dream was sent by God?"

"Absolutely, Antoni. Every thought that passes through a man's head comes from God, from God's own heart. God almighty is the father of all of our thoughts, and our dreams as well. What is a dream but God's word in disguise?"

"If you ask me, Nikodem, I say we should steer clear of danger. Poles shouldn't get mixed up in a fight between the Germans and the Jews. I did help a Jew once, long ago when the Germans first arrived. I helped him escape the village. And to this very day, the people in my village give me strange looks. Let me ask you this: What if the stranger got caught by a German? What would happen then?"

"Antoni, it's the darkest hour of night right *now*. Can't you hear the storm outside? Now is the time. God Himself has sent me a message."

The ancient bell ringer rose from his bed and wrapped himself in his coat. All the while, Antoni did not take his eyes from the window, where the snowstorm knocked with broken white wings. The two old men descended the narrow spiral staircase and entered the church sanctuary. It was pitch-black except for a thin strip of moonlight shining through the snow-covered stained glass. But Nikodem needed no light; he knew every nook and cranny of the sanctuary. He grabbed the peasant with his right hand and pulled him along until they reached the altar.

There they stopped and listened for any sound from the cellar. Nothing could be heard besides the blizzard howling outside. Dawn was still a long way off, tucked away in the darkness of the night. The bell ringer was sure the hour was propitious. They hoped to hear something in the cellar, maybe the strange man breathing in his sleep. But still there was nothing, only the patter of mice skittering by on the other side of the wall. The mice cried out and took refuge behind the wooden cross.

Nikodem reached into a drawer inside the altar and pulled out a white cassock.

"This will help him get across the field—Father Jankowski's cassock."

Then he knelt down, slid back the rug, and slowly lifted the trapdoor. They leaned over the dark opening and waited anxiously for a sign.

"Stranger! Stranger!" The bell ringer called out into the darkness.

Not the slightest sound came from below.

"Hello? Hello? Please answer. We've come to help you."

And then, finally, a weak voice could be heard.

"Who's there?" he asked in Polish.

"Listen, stranger. It's me and my neighbor. Don't be afraid. It's time for you to go. It's dangerous to stay here. We'll show you the shortest way to get to the ghetto. It's just across the field. God in heaven will help you and protect you."

Antoni whispered a few words of encouragement. Then they both told the stranger to hurry, warning him of the imminent sunrise over the ghetto fields. Finally the Jew emerged from the darkness. He stood between the old men like a dark pillar. It was impossible to make out the contours of his body, neither his hands nor his head. If they had not heard his rapid breathing, they wouldn't have believed he'd risen from the cellar and was standing before them. They realized then that he was shivering in the cold. The two old men suddenly felt the stranger clutch their arms. His hands felt heavy and icy. The three of them stood there for a few moments in complete silence, as the snow continued to strike against the stained-glass windows and the wind roared over the uppermost vault of the church.

The bell ringer opened up the white cassock and quickly wrapped it around the stranger. Antoni held the sleeves and helped his hands through. The white robe seemed made for the stranger; he was tall and lean, just like Father Jankowski. The cassock draped down to just above his feet. Now the dark pillar that had appeared between the two men was transformed into a white silhouette, as if touched by the dawning sun.

The bell ringer led the stranger through the courtyard to the back door, which looked out on the ghetto. As they walked, he spoke to the stranger in rapid whispers, telling him how to reach the ghetto cemetery fence without running into trouble. This was the safest time, before dawn, while the guards were dozing in their watchtowers. As soon as he made it across the potato fields behind the church, he would have to turn left and crawl on the ground behind the broken-down, abandoned building. That would be a good place to stop and rest. From there, the field sloped downward. He would have to stick to the downward grade to avoid getting off track. It would be hard to see anything, even the German guard post, now that the snow was so deep. The field was also pockmarked with numerous deep holes, which he would have to avoid.

"But the storm is a gift sent from heaven to keep you out of view. Remember to rest at the abandoned building. And, when you get down the hill, you'll find a deep crevice under the barbed-wire fence. But don't move until you hear the signal."

"The signal?" the stranger murmured weakly. It was the first time the old men had heard his voice clearly. It hardly sounded human, more like the voice of a spirit speaking from the netherworld.

"Yes. Don't go under the barbed-wire fence until you hear the church bells ringing in the tower. The bells will be your signal that it's safe to cross. The sound of the bells will mask the noise of the fence. The German guards are used to hearing the church bells at night."

As the stranger turned and started down the steps, the bell ringer reached out and held him for a moment. He made the sign of the cross above the figure in the white cassock. Antoni bowed and whispered the words of a prayer.

✦

With the white cassock fluttering around him, the stranger ran from the church to the potato field. The storm was blowing violently from the north. He reached the potato field and lay on the cold ground, holding his breath. He kept repeating in his mind the bell ringer's instructions: *left at the abandoned building, down the sloping hill; the graveyard's a hundred steps away.* The Jews were just on the other side of the fence—it was there he would fulfill his mission.

He wrapped his cassock tightly around himself against the cold and lay down between two furrows in the barren field. The storm raged above. Just ahead of him, he saw the crumbling building. A thin ray of light shone through one of the cracks in the wall. He raised his head and met the sharp, icy edges of falling snowflakes. Turning around, he gazed back at the church tower, now shrouded in mist. There, in the church, he'd been kept safe. While waiting in the cellar, he'd regained his strength, along with his faith in his task. How restless he had been to leave the dank, dark cellar. His sense of mission had driven him onward like the burning lash of a whip. Sometimes he'd feared that he would arrive too late, that he would no longer meet any Jews on the other side of the fence. But regardless of the risks, he had left the cellar with great energy and resolve, and now he felt indescribable joy to be under the open sky, showered by the falling snow. Such a large, expansive, free sky! How strange that he should feel so free, so safe, nestled among snowy furrows, wearing a white robe that blended in with the white of the snow. The darkness of night seemed to lend him tremendous power, the icy snowflakes on his lips summoning latent reserves of strength. At this moment of absolute peril, he was guided by one task: to reach the Jews beyond the fence, to reach the Jews, to reach the Jews, to reach the Jews.

Suddenly fatigue washed over him. He collapsed onto the snowy ground, numb from the cold. His hands were impossibly heavy, as were his eyelids, which he struggled to keep open. The building he was heading toward loomed before him like a nocturnal creature. He panicked at the thought that he'd missed the signal from the bell tower. Had it already rung and he'd been too numb to hear? How long had he now been outside, in the furrows of the frozen potato field? Could the sound of bells pierce the roar of the storm?

He started crawling again and finally reached the crumbling structure. It must have once been some kind of forge; now it was in ruins. He curled up next to the wall, which protected him from the watchtower. It hadn't been so hard to reach it. Looking backward over the snowy field, he could see how far he'd come. The church tower loomed in the distance, shrouded by the falling snow. The tower. The tower. The white tower . . .

With the wind roaring in his ears, he saw a thick, black object jutting out from the brick wall. It was an old piece of iron, probably part of an axle or a scythe of some kind. He pried it loose and discovered a pool of melted snow, which he poured into his cupped hands and drank. Just then, a band of white light flashed out from the north. He was sure it was a German searchlight panning over the ghetto fence, but it turned out to be a ray of moonlight escaping from behind a dark cloud. The stranger turned back and saw the church tower illuminated. It gleamed in the winter moonlight, its roof glistening like polished bones. Though it lasted a mere instant, the illumination seemed like a miraculous vision. Then the tower vanished, engulfed in the darkness of night. The storm had picked up again, howling like a madman and lashing the stranger's face.

Just then, a thin, metallic sound pierced the night sky like a distant lament. The stranger pushed himself up from the snowy ground with his elbows; he was ready to make the final push. The church bells rang out across the dark fields. They rang out louder and louder, a heavy, echoing herald pouring forth from the invisible tower.

14

The Rope

The Marysin train station lay huddled in the snow just beyond the eastern edge of the ghetto. For several weeks now, groups of Polish peasants appeared there every morning at dawn. They came from all around Łagiewniki, as far as Głowno and the small villages on the banks of the Bzura River, on the border of Łęczyca district. They wore gloomy expressions as they marched along, wrapped in tattered blankets and ragged sheepskin coats, their feet barely protected by old wooden clogs. They assembled first in open fields or behind churches or on the steps of town halls, or even in cemeteries. From there, they would be led by armed German officers, the SS, and the Polish police force across the fields past the ghetto to the station. There, platform wagons waited, filled with black rails. At the first light of dawn, never-ending lines of peasants would haul the rails from the wagons and carry them across the fields. A sinister metallic clanging reverberated through the ghetto. Small teams of peasants would dig into the frozen earth with shovels and pickaxes, leveling the hills and laying down the wooden supports, while other teams would bring the shiny rails and fit them into place. With each new day the tracks gained more and more ground. The steel arms reached around the eastern border of the ghetto, through bare fields, meadows, and sparse pine groves. They passed tiny villages and finally arrived at the big railway junction on the western side of the ghetto.

Rumors spread through the villages and towns about the purpose of the Germans' new tracks. It was already several weeks after Yuletide, the frigid days of February 1944. At night, the frozen windows of peasant houses would shake as freight trains rumbled through the forest. They were coming from the forests near the Bug River. The trains only traveled at night. Throughout the Łagiewniki region, peasants' hearts swelled with the dream of liberation, an end to the war. They knew that the trains coming from the East were filled with German soldiers, military supplies, and weapons. They could hear explosions in the forests of Łęczyca. Partisans were hurling grenades and homemade missiles at the German trains. Old men who had been spared deportation to German labor camps exulted whenever they heard a detonation. They saw the new tracks extending from the East as proof the Germans were preparing to withdraw from Poland. Others claimed the tracks would be used to deport the last remaining Jews from the ghetto.

Clouds of thick gray fog shrouded the northern end of the city, but when the peasants looked down from the surrounding hilltops, they could still see the empty ghetto fields behind the Jewish graveyards. They also saw the only church in the ghetto, the Church of the Assumption of the Blessed Virgin Mary, its tower piercing the heavy clouds. On clear days, they could make out the bell-tower clock, with its unmoving hands, and the sharp tongues of the gargoyles, sending mocking laughter to the four corners of the world.

For the Kaczmareks as well, these changes seemed clear signs that the end was near. Even as they frantically sorted through their stash of Jewish possessions in the attic, they could hear trains coming from the East. They had to complete their work as soon as possible. More than once, the Germans had threatened severe punishment for anybody caught stealing Jewish property—clothes, shoes, blankets, anything made of silver or gold, even cooking utensils. Everything left behind by Jews, whether those sent into the ghetto or deported, was considered property of the Reich to be sent either back to Germany or to the occupied regions. In truth, Stefan considered it a miracle that everything had gone as smoothly as it had up to that point. But now that Commander Jessicke was dead and they had received word that the inn had to be abandoned, he understood that the good times were over. What worried the Kaczmareks most was their neighbor in the Church of Saint Francis, old Nikodem Załucki. He knew what they had been up to, he'd seen the boxes filled with clothes heading in the back door. More than once, he'd hinted as much to Stefan. The old man didn't support the new regime—he'd never accepted Hitler's new order in Poland and all the territories the Reich controlled.

But now everything was about to change again. Stefan didn't know what to make of all the rumors, he only knew one thing: the most dangerous person for *him* was none other than Nikodem Załucki. Of course, it was no surprise that the old man was untrustworthy—if you had a son fooling around with the partisans, you were probably no better yourself. Ah, but what Załucki had hidden under the altar—that was Stefan's greatest asset. As soon as morning broke, he'd sneak into the church along with a German guard. He'd slide back the rug and *pow!* You can't kill the hare without a shot. He would drag that Żyd out by his curly mop. And then, then the dangerous bell ringer wouldn't be so dangerous anymore. Just wait. Ha! God always sent the remedy just before the plague.

Stefan grinned in anticipation, caressing the velvet tefillin bag he had hidden in his pocket.

✦

By the time the first rays of dawn appeared in the eastern sky, the snowstorm had died down. Only the razor-sharp wind remained. The sun broke through the sky, crowned by a blazing halo. The wind stirred up shimmering flurries of snow, but today there was no threat of a new storm.

Nikodem had long since sounded the morning bells and folded up the straw sack Antoni used as a bed. Now he was sitting in the chapel, drinking his bitter coffee. He watched through the window as Antoni vanished into the Łagiewniki woods on his horse-drawn cart. Everything had gone according to plan. With his hands resting on the windowsill, he let his eyes wander over the blue horizon. It was already an hour since the sun had risen, the stranger was long gone, and Nikodem felt safe. The cellar beneath the altar was empty. Let them come and see. After all, what had he done but helped a man in distress? Was it really so extraordinary? It was all the will of God.

Absorbed by these thoughts, he could make out the contours of several men on the road from the forest. From Nikodem's perch by the window, the men looked like small shadows running toward the church. He leaned forward to see more clearly. Smiling to himself, he whispered, "Oh, *Boże*, eternal God in heaven, you have shown me great mercy. The dream you sent me was a sign indeed. Now I see it has all come true."

He hurried down the steps into the sanctuary, opened the outside door, and stood at the threshold waiting. The empty courtyard in front of the church was blanketed in snow, while in the field beyond patches of earth peeked out at the early morning sun. In about a month's time, he reflected, the sun would melt the snow and green shoots would spring up everywhere. He glanced at the outermost corner of the courtyard, where the two Jewish children had been buried. The solitary tree standing just opposite their graves looked more majestic than ever, its crown radiant. The long branches dragged along the earth, as if seeking to quench their thirst with the melting snow.

Now he saw the approaching men clearly; they were just beyond the field. One of them, he could tell, was Stefan Kaczmarek. He was running behind two German guards. They would arrive at the church courtyard in a matter of moments. Standing still in the open doorway, the old man crossed himself.

The Germans, in their heavy fur coats, came to stand directly before him, their steel helmets flashing a reddish glow. With a kick of their boots, they pushed open the church door, which had closed behind the bell ringer. They strode into the church, followed by Kaczmarek, who lowered his head as if out of respect, all the while casting oblique glances at Nikodem.

The old man followed them inside without speaking. He felt calm, though his quavering eyes betrayed a deep-seated hatred for these men. As he watched them, he realized his hatred for Kaczmarek was even stronger. After all, Germans and Poles had always been enemies, and these soldiers were merely fighting for their fatherland. But what could be said for Stefan Kaczmarek? A Polish woman had given birth to him, nursed him; the Polish land had sustained him, provided his daily bread. All this so he could serve Poland's greatest enemy? No, no, not so fast, you son of a . . .

Meanwhile, the three men walked down the aisle and stopped just before the altar. Stefan glanced around at the empty church. Bright rays of sunlight streamed through the stained-glass windows. The wooden crucifix together with the severed arm of Saint Francis of Assisi were illuminated by a beam of warm light. The German who was closest to the altar bent down, rolled up the rug, and opened the trapdoor with great meticulousness. Then he signaled to Stefan, who leapt into the cellar.

A heavy silence fell over the church, as the German took out his flashlight and shone it over the dank basement into which Stefan had just disappeared. The stillness was terrifying. Tense breathing echoed softly through the church. Wind rushed in from a broken window, blowing past the plaster heads of saints. Standing behind the Germans, the bell ringer fixed his eyes on the folds of their necks. They were bright red, as if filled with an excess of blood and fat. The one with the flashlight stared with a look of uncertainty into the open trapdoor.

Stefan burst out of the cellar clutching an empty wine bottle. He was holding something else besides. The bell ringer strained his eyes. What could it be? Now he perceived a strange object that he had never seen before. Stefan raised the bottle high above his head and waved it around triumphantly. The bell ringer looked on with glazed eyes, as his body shook. He felt his fate descend on him like a noose.

The German who'd been kneeling stood and let out a cry that resounded like a wolf's howl at night.

"Where is the Jude? Who was it that drank this wine, huh?"

The bell ringer broke into a smile and murmured something. Stefan translated it into German.

"He says it's just an old bottle. No Jude . . . No Jude at all . . ."

Stefan planted himself in front of the bell ringer, his deep-set eyes ablaze with fury.

"And what's this, old man?" He waved a little bag in front of Nikodem. "Don't we have proof right here that you hid a Jew, a damned Żyd?"

Stunned, the bell ringer saw a wrinkled velvet bag in the red palm of Stefan's hand. The bag was open, revealing black leather straps inside. Slowly, the German picked up the straps and examined them. Then he removed the boxes from their cases, squeezing them in his pointy fingers. The straps dangled to the floor, quivering as if in fear. The black boxes looked like a palpable emblem of the Jews' dark fate.

The bell ringer bowed his head in defeat. Something he'd never imagined had just come to pass. Oh God, why hadn't it occurred to him to look through the cellar after the stranger left? How could he have forgotten the bottle of holy wine he'd given him? And, at the last minute, had the stranger forgotten to take with him his strange Jewish bag?

Old Nikodem couldn't take his eyes off the shiny black tefillin. His eyelids were shaking. He had never before seen the secret objects of the Jews. How they shimmered in the winter light. He looked up at the wall and fixed his gaze on the crucifix with the figure of the Savior. Suddenly he imagined that the deep blackness of the Jewish boxes had painted itself on the forehead of the crucified Christ. Shafts of sunlight filtered through the window and rested on Jesus's shoulders, transforming before Nikodem's eyes into the black leather straps dangling from the strange Jewish boxes. There they hung, down to the skeletal feet nailed to the cross. The bell ringer no longer saw the men who stood before him near the open cellar door. He could not even hear the vicious words they hurled at him. It seemed to him that the cellar at the foot of the altar had just opened its door for him, and that soon he would plunge into the abyss.

✦

A few days passed. Sunday morning sparkled in the clear blue light pouring from the eastern Polish skies. The earth had begun to free itself from the snow, and dark patches seemed to luxuriate in the warm sun. Islands of grass that survived the winter were visible in the pools of sunlight beneath sparse pine trees. During the night, the flowing waters of the Bzura broke through the river's frozen shield. All that remained were shiny strips of ice, which looked like silver-plated mirrors as they floated downstream, heading toward the greening valleys of Mazovia. As the returning birds glided over the river, their shadows on the floating chunks of ice looked like fallen leaves drifting along in the current.

The peaceful Sunday morning was interrupted by the relentless, heavy clanging of church bells. It began early, before the first rays of dawn had appeared in the east. This was not the customary tolling of the bells for Sunday Mass. Instead, the bells were an official summons, issued to all the villagers throughout the Łagiewniki region. Whole families poured onto the roads heading to the forest. Peasant women, old men, and children, along with a few young men, made their way along the narrow paths, which had just been liberated from the snow. Some of the villagers traveled in horse-drawn carts and wagons. Most went on foot. All were heading to an open field just beyond the woods, near the northern border of the ghetto.

A few days earlier, the Germans had nailed up placards in every marketplace, church, and tavern, ordering the population to appear that Sunday morning at the Church of Saint Francis. Those who disobeyed would be severely punished. Such orders were always a bad sign. They had probably caught another Jew trying to escape from the ghetto, or maybe it was a Pole who'd run away from a German labor camp. Usually the suspect had been caught carrying a weapon. And generally, whenever the Germans ordered the local residents to appear, it was to remind them of the punishment that awaited anyone found to be an enemy of the Reich.

The peasants came dressed in their Sunday best, but the mood was somber. With heads bowed, the men trailed behind the women and children riding on wagons. The Łagiewniki district covered an area of several kilometers, stretching all the way to Łęczyca. So many people appeared that an observer might have thought it was a return to the old days, when the faithful used to crowd the roads leading to the shrine at Jasna Góra. More and more people joined the throngs as they pressed onward in silent procession.

As the road sloped downward, the horses picked up their pace. Now that the snow had begun to melt and the dark earth was exposed, their pounding hooves sent the mud flying. The wheels of the carriages and hay wagons dug ever-deepening grooves in the road. Pious women and girls lifted flags emblazoned with church insignia above the crowd. Priests marched in their vestments, with their knitted hats and with heavy crosses around their necks. When the first crowds reached the church, the sun was already high in the sky. The church filled quickly with people; the rest gradually squeezed into the square. The tall white belfries kept guard over the gathering crowd. Standing pressed together, everyone looked toward the field stretching before the ghetto fence. A group of pale-faced priests stood in front of the lone tree in the church courtyard. Two Germans in green uniforms stood by a table, flipping through sheets of paper and glancing nervously at their watches. The crowd left an open space immediately around them. They glanced back and forth between the white tower and the ghetto fence. A long, braided rope dangled from the tower, swaying in the wind. The sun was now directly over the tower, and the bell at the top was lit up like a shining orb.

Suddenly, the sea of heads turned to the north as if in a single motion. Something was happening in the field just outside the ghetto. A car had appeared, driving slowly toward the courtyard. It looked like a shiny, black casket with tiny windows at the rear. Everyone's eyes followed the car as it approached the courtyard, cut through the throngs of people, and stopped in front of the tree.

A silence fell over the crowd. The only sound in the courtyard came from the church banners flapping in the wind.. Everyone seemed to hold their breath. A number of peasant women, anticipating what was about to happen, dropped to their knees and began praying. Two priests passed in front of the crowd and looked in the back windows of the car. It was clear to everyone that the car was carrying a Jew who'd tried to escape. These wretched people had more than once been brought to squares and marketplaces before being hanged at the gallows. No, there was no doubt this had to do with that ghetto where the Jews were locked up. Soon the condemned Jew would emerge from the car, and then everyone would see what the Germans had in store.

At the far edge of the courtyard stood an old, mossy oak, bent over as if in fatigue and resignation. The thick branches were bare by the trunk, but early foliage was sprouting near the top. Its leaves were dark green, outlined by a few lonely sparks of gold. When the peasants raised their eyes to the top of the tree, they saw a flat shape that looked like a straw hat turned upside down: it was the nest of a long-departed stork. In their weary hearts, the peasants felt the abandoned nest was a perfect image for Poland's devastation. They kept their eyes on the top of the oak until one of the Germans ran to the church tower and seized the rope. He shortened it with a quick slice of his knife. The sudden movement shook the bells, which murmured over the stunned crowd.

When the German returned with the rope, someone opened the door of the car. A short, hunched figure rose and stood near the tree. He gazed at the crowd, listening to the faint clanging of the bells, which he heard echoing long after anyone else did. He stood for a while in silence, his head bent over. Those who stood near him could see that his eyes were half-closed, giving him an almost peaceful appearance. When they recognized him, everyone let out a horrified gasp. He looked smaller than usual, but it was unmistakably Nikodem Załucki, the old bell ringer from the Church of Saint Francis of Assisi. He turned his head upward and gazed toward the tower, as the German placed the rope in his hand. One of the Germans stood up on the table and began shouting at the crowd. He pointed at the condemned man, who, rather than serving God and Jesus Christ, had decided instead to serve a Jew! In the innermost sanctuary of his holy church, this one went and hid a Jew! Here was an empty bottle of sacred wine that the Jew drank, and here were the straps that the devil used to say his secret prayers. These were the evil ropes that the Jews placed around the necks of all Christians, all Germans, the whole world—to strangle us! *Heil Hitler!*

High above his head, the German brandished the empty bottle and the tefillin straps. He wanted everyone to see the evidence for themselves. The peasants nearest to the tree knelt down. A man was about to be hanged on the gallows, right before their eyes. A priest approached old Nikodem and whispered something into his ear. Then the German leapt down from the table and slapped the bell ringer on the cheek with the tefillin straps.

All the while, the bell ringer clutched the rope. He had a look of detachment, almost serenity. It occurred to him that over all these years serving the church, all these years pulling this very rope, he had never really inspected it. As it lay in his leathery hands, he stared at it now with an intense focus. It looked strange: it wasn't quite black, but braided with a mix of thin gray, black, and white strands. He noticed the weave had come undone at parts, and threads were protruding at odd intervals. The threads shone in the sunlight. The thought that all these countless years he had pulled this very rope, that this rope had in turn pulled the bell in the tower so many times—this thought gave him a sudden feeling of joy, incomprehensible joy. And it had helped *him*—the stranger—when he needed to escape. And now it was going around the bell ringer's neck. Here under the green oak.

The old man was slowly led to the tree. He stood in the wide black shadows cast by the heavy, low-hanging branches. From far away, he looked like a bird swaying backward on spindly legs, waiting to take flight. Soon the bird would spread his huge tremulous wings and soar off on a distant journey to a long, peaceful, shadowy sleep.

15

Secrets of the Mound

Soft winds blew through the windows and cracked wooden doorframes. With the beginning of the month of Nisan, the final spring in the ghetto had begun.

A group of women and young girls were sitting around a mound of dirty potato skins in a garbage shed behind the soup kitchen. The mound gave off warm steam as if from its secret entrails; the steam floated upward and hovered around the ceiling, where it vibrated in the bluish light like the strings of an instrument. It was as if a song of light, played on an invisible violin, were drifting above the women's bent heads.

The garbage shed stood at the edge of the courtyard, near the locked, worm-eaten gate. Inside, the dark mound cast a mezmerizing spell. The women sat in a circle, some on crumbling bricks, others on the floor, all with their bare legs crossed. They huddled together like a mysterious sisterhood engaged in an exorcism. They didn't seem to notice the foul-smelling fumes wafting above their heads, hovering in a white mist barely illumined by the dim light hanging from the ceiling. With repetitive hand motions, they reached for the mound and sifted through dark brown lumps. Sometimes they would find a treasure: an edible piece of a withered potato. The mound was dark and sticky, with holes carved into its sides that seemed to magically attract the outstretched hands of the women and girls.

No one spoke as they performed their labor; their sunken eyes were often closed. It was only when the mound was nearly hollowed out and a few scattered potato peels were all that remained that someone let out a sigh, though whether it sought to convey relief or desperation was impossible to tell. Maybe the women sifting through the potatoes were not even human, but unearthly beings who'd descended from the mound to perform secret rites in the darkness. They bowed their heads toward the mound, and when they reached inside it, their hands seemed to be caught in one of the holes, until, by a rocking gesture of their whole body, they managed to free themselves again.

As the women carried out their desperate search for edible scraps in the garbage shed, the first fragrant winds of the Polish spring were stirring in the outside world. The winds blew in from the open field beyond the fence, where tufts of yellow grass still grew, refusing to yield to death. The winds swept over the broken walls, bringing a scent of distant orchards through cracks in the roof of the garbage shed. The women raised their heads and breathed in the new aromas, inhaling deeply as if trying to quench their thirst.

"My friends, my *likhtike*, I think it's finally—"

"Oh, sure, that's how they talk about the Messiah."

"No, no. I think she's right, seems like this time—"

"You're all crazy! Ought to keep your mouths shut."

"Hush!"

"Did you catch that smell? It's already—"

"What smell?"

"A sweet smell—oh, it's been so long."

"A smell?"

"Yes, my girls, yes, that smell."

"It smells like pears."

"Pears? The pears of Nisan?"

"Yes, no mistaking that smell. I swear to God, I even smell apples."

"It smells like someone's building a fire."

As if in a single motion, the women removed their hands from the mound of potato peels and focused on the sounds and smells outside. The mound itself looked like a secret source of important knowledge that was on the verge of being revealed. But it withheld whatever truths it contained and now appeared to be listening in the darkness, just like the assembled women. The sweet scents of early spring wafted through the shed. They could hear the chirping of a cricket—somewhere far away.

"Pears! Real pears! Can you believe it?"

"Come on, stop being ridiculous. How could there possibly be real pears?"

"Why not? They grow in the orchards all around here. *They* have plenty of pears."

"Yes, it's like magic. They've got magic trees."

"Magic? Ha, ha!"

They breathed in the scent once again, opening their mouths as if to taste the fresh fruit. But just as quickly as it had appeared, the sweet aroma dissipated. A harsh wind blew into the shed, mocking the women, who turned back in defeat to their work. They sat in silence, hunting through the potato skins for a few meager treasures. And when the room succumbed to darkness and they could no longer see one another, they abandoned all restraint, sucking on the cold, rotten potato peels, which lay in their mouths like shards of glass.

Over the low roof of the garbage shed, a full moon appeared in the sky, heralding the arrival of Passover. It was enveloped in countless strands of fog that seemed to bind it to the stars of the Milky Way. Radiant clouds gathered in the eastern part of the sky, where the moon had risen. The silvery moonlight lit up the northern side of the ghetto, while the rest of the area slumbered on in darkness. The distant glow from the Milky Way scattered countless tiny sparks on the ground, and even the garbage shed filled with a silvery light.

"Have you heard what they're saying, girls?"

"What are they saying, sweetheart?"

"They're saying, God willing, they're saying that—"

All heads turned toward the woman who was speaking.

"Please tell us, *tayrinke*."

"They say tomorrow there'll be a shipment into the ghetto."

Everyone pulled their hands from the mound of potato skins.

"What kind of shipment?"

"What are you talking about?"

"Bones. God willing, bones—"

"Bones?"

"Yes, that's what I'm telling you. Bones. Did you hear what happened to that crazy violinist?"

"What violinist?

"They say he was from Czechoslovakia, from Prague. He hid his violin somewhere. What a lunatic."

"Who could possibly need a violin in the ghetto? Unless he's completely insane."

"They say he was part of the resistance, with the radio."

Suddenly, silence fell. The last person to speak burst into tears.

"Why are you crying, *tayrinke*? It's terrible for every one of us. Someone should cry for us all."

A wavering voice could be heard on the other side of the mound.

"They say someone snitched on them. I knew it was dangerous for them to keep that radio."

"What? Who snitched?"

"There's no shortage of Jewish traitors in the ghetto. So why not?"

"They shouldn't have risked their lives. The end is so near, any day now. What a tragedy for our boys."

"They said he used his violin case to attack the Germans."

"One of them even had a bayonet."

"How could a Jew get his hands on a bayonet?"

"And that one of them poisoned himself. Do you believe *that*, *tayrinke*?"

"Poisoned?"

"That's what they're saying. They found him in a doorway—somewhere on Hotelowa Street; he was already dead. He was from my town, you know—he was one of the Vidaver group."

"Better one death than ten, God forbid."

"*Vey iz undz!* And I'll tell you who's to blame. It's all *that one's* fault, the one the German bastards picked up near the graveyard. Remember? Just after the last big snowstorm."

"Nonsense! The Germans didn't need him to find them. The Kripo had enough informers without him . . ."

"Those damned rats!"

"Did you say that old man handed him over to the Germans himself?"

"That's what they say. Who was it who got caught? Was he one of us?"

"They say he was from somewhere else."

"Was he a Jew?"

"Who knows? I only saw him that awful Saturday. It was at the fish market. He was hanging by that rope all day, wearing some kind of a white robe, you couldn't even see his face."

The voices in the garbage shed went silent once again. Outside, the crickets started up their raspy lament. The women continued their work, sifting quickly through potato skins and tossing them back on the ground.

"Did you say bones? God willing."

"Yes, bones. Real bones."

"How do you know it's really bones, sweetheart?"

"I heard it myself—from the Bat . . ."

"Ha! What does the Bat really know?"

"Well why shouldn't he know? Who else if not the Bat? Let's ask Gitele. She's been going around with him. They're joined at the hip. Gitele, tell us, is it true that there's going to be a shipment of bones?"

Gitele was sitting in the circle of women with her head lowered; she did not answer. Her hands were covered in dirt. The threat lurking in the garbage shed chatter was now out in the open, as if a little demon with cloven feet had crawled out of the mound and hopped around in front of her, wielding a tiny whip and hissing at her. She felt as if the air in the shed had become electrified. The women stuck out their tongues and began licking themselves like massive, ghostly cats.

"Tell me this, where would the Germans get bones to ship to the Jews in the ghetto?"

"Yeah, where? Tell me that."

"From their horses! Their horses . . . Do you think there's any shortage of horses?"

"Horses?"

"What else? It couldn't be from cows or calves."

"You girls are all being silly. The Germans are probably using the horsemeat to feed their own troops. After five years of war, there's hardly anything left. So they're eating their horses. See? And they'll leave us the bones."

"God forbid! What will we do with bones?"

"They're real bones, that's what I'm telling you."

"Oh my God, it just occurred to me that maybe they're human bones. Bones of Jews. Oh my God!"

"Quiet that witch down! Who says they're human bones? Don't you remember how last year they brought us bones? I myself got a veal bone. I recognized the taste. I swear by the Messiah himself."

"Oh, *vey iz tsu undz,* how we suffer."

Dusk settled outside, and the moon disappeared into the darkness. The air in the garbage shed was dense and sticky. Gitele remained silent as the women removed their hands from the mound of potato skins. They waited motionless for the sound of knocking on the wall, the signal from the Bat that it was time to place the potato chunks they'd found in the big black pot and return home.

✦

Behind the infernal black barrels in the soup kitchen, Vigdor was lying shirtless on a low cot, gently stroking an old cat. The cat was round and plump, resting on Vigdor's broad hairy torso like a child. The cat's coarse whiskers stuck out like the needles of a pine tree. Its green eyes cast an infernal glow into the darkness of the room. The cat had become accustomed to spending long hours lying across Vigdor's body, sometimes burying its snout in his hairy chest.

The Bat—nobody remembered when the women started calling Vigdor that, but the name stuck—had discovered the cat when it was still very small and liked to hide behind the trash bin, near a cracked window where the cool air came in from the ghetto courtyard. It was just after Vigdor returned from Gestapo headquarters, where they had beaten him soundly. He brought the cat with him to keep him company whenever he stood guard in the shed at night. Vigdor's body no longer exuded the strength it had just a few months earlier. It was now disfigured by hunger and the beatings. The pointy tip of his chin jutted out like the head of a violin, his pencil-thin arms dangled like the wings of a startled bird, and his wan face was covered with a mangy beard. Hair had grown on his neck and arms as well, and the women avoided him as if he were a demon. If he startled a girl in the middle of the street, he would wave his hands to reassure her that he was human. Nobody knew exactly where the Bat spent his days. Some said he hid out by the gravestones and crypts in the cemetery. One woman saw him build a shelter there, along with a web of nets he used to catch birds. The Bat would attract them by imitating their calls. Then he would poke out their eyes with a needle and listen to their death song. And what he did next with the birds was truly astounding. Ever since the great hunger, the Bat would enter the dark crypts of famous rabbis and boil the dead birds. Then he would bring the broth to sick and dying people throughout the ghetto. One of the women from the soup kitchen swore that the Bat had healed her dying husband. After drinking a bowl of his broth, the husband had stood up from his deathbed and started walking around, saying he felt fine. Some of the women said that on nights when they couldn't sleep, they would look into the windows of the garbage shed and see the Bat playing with the cat next to the fireplace. When day broke, he'd vanish. Then, with the coming of dusk, he'd reappear in the shed, along with his cat, and resume his nocturnal existence.

And so, since the great disaster, Vigdor and the little cat had entered into an unspoken pact. They spent their nights together and went their separate ways at daybreak. Whenever Vigdor was in the kitchen, he liked to lie back and whistle a meandering, haunting tune that was sometimes so loud it seemed to shake the wooden walls. When it was too much for the women working through the potato skins, they would bang on the wall and yell at him to stop in their raspy, desperate voices.

"Hey Bat, stop tormenting us with your damned song. Leave us in peace."

"It sounds like the Devil's caught you. *Ptui, ptui . . .*"

"Graveyard man, did you marry your cat?"

"He's been eating those dirty birds!"

"Believe me, he wasn't born to a Jewish mother. Gitele, can't you shut up the Bat?"

When he heard Gitele's name pronounced in the adjoining room, Vigdor would suddenly fall silent. Then he would rise and press his head against the wall to discern the voice, like a bird suspended before its night prey. Sometimes he would poke his head into the dimly lit room and fix his gaze on Gitele as she reached her hands into the slimy mound and pulled them out again, her fingers flashing before his eyes like tiny beams of white light.

Vigdor liked to scare the women by making all sorts of animal and bird noises. Most of all he liked to project his voice over Gitele's head in high-pitched melodies as if he were a songbird in flight. He knew how to imitate the trilling of a canary and the whistling of the Polish starlings that collected in summer bushes. He would wait until it had gone quiet in the garbage shed, when all the women seemed to be listening to the outside world, then surprise them with his birdcalls and his whistling. All the while, the cat would be perched on his shoulders, its green eyes shining like phosphorescent light. Finally, Vigdor would tire of his game and, drifting away from the dark corner like a black fish, he would lie down again on his cot behind the black barrels.

16

Bones

One evening, a wooden cart rolled into the courtyard near the soup kitchen. It was covered with a coarse black tarpaulin and the wheels looked like they'd been taken from a toy wagon. One man pushed the cart, while a crowd of people followed closely behind, keeping their hungry eyes fixed on it as it rumbled over the cobblestones. From under the tarpaulin rose a jagged form, as if the elbows of a corpse were jutting upward. The women from the garbage shed stood on either side of the cart, holding it steady as it went. They wore black kerchiefs around their heads and shoulders, as if in a funeral procession, but their expressions hinted that there were no corpses beneath the tarpaulin, but some sort of treasure. Vigdor raced up and down the side streets, springing into the air and calling people into the courtyard.

"I told you! I told you, good women, we'd have bones."

"Real bones?"

The cart moved slowly through a narrow passageway and entered the next courtyard, where it stopped on a dirt path that had turned to mud weeks earlier in the spring rain. Everyone remained silent, resting their hands on their hips. Their eyes shone with anticipation. The protrusions under the tarpaulin had rearranged themselves, and now looked like arms reaching out in every direction.

"Bones, God be praised. Praise to the Eternal One. Jews, give thanks to His name. We've got bones. Real bones!"

The whispering voices of women repeated the word *bones* as if it were a magical incantation capable of restoring life to the bones under the black cover.

Suddenly, the cat from the garbage shed appeared out of the darkness and came leaping through the air. In one bound, it landed on top of the load of bones on the cart.

"Pssst! Pssst! Psssssst!" The women shook their kerchiefs and apron strings at the cat. "Pssst! You see that devil? He's sniffing the bones. Psst! Scram! Get lost!"

But the cat didn't move. Instead it opened its mouth and slowly turned to Vigdor with an almost pensive look. Then it licked its lips and surveyed the crowd. Its eyes glistened like those of a demon. The women backed away in fear, wrapped their shawls tightly around their bodies, and waited for the Bat to shoo the cat away.

Meanwhile Vigdor lifted the black tarpaulin little by little, and when it was uncovered, the women rushed in, trying to focus their eyes in the dim light. The cart was filled to the brim with a profusion of bones—black, reddish, gray pink, and pale blue. Narrow tendrils of frozen blood extended from the tips in narrow lines. Some of the bones were pale, like the cheeks of dying men, while others were covered in a thin, milky-white veneer that looked like patches of flayed skin. All were tossed about and chipped, sometimes with a crack down the middle exposing pink marrow.

The women stared at the strange shapes before them. It looked as if some indiscriminate violent force had waged a battle inside the closed world of the wagon. Limbs had been torn apart, skulls cracked. Pointed elbows were left extending outward, as if in a last, desperate cry for mercy. The only sound came from the wind blowing over the avalanche of bones, which rattled like the strings of a broken lyre. And now it seemed that the black arm of death was reaching out to them from beneath the stack of bones. The human body was powerless before such a violent force—everything in its path was destined to lie humiliated and bare.

✦

Whenever she picked through the mound of potato skins, Gitele took great care to protect her right hand, above all her slim, feminine fingers. She only used her left hand, which had become swollen and hardened as if covered in a brown glove. Her right hand, by contrast, was still supple. It looked like her hands belonged to two different people. The women in the garbage shed teased her, saying she was keeping her right hand pure for the abandoned child she was taking care of.

Gitele was now living across from the shed in a small room perched on the top floor like a bird's nest. Wind, snow, and rain pounded the sloping roof, and narrow tufts of grass and even wildflowers were beginning to grow in the cracks between the slats and the bricks. Though the path through the courtyard remained devoid of any life, the Polish spring was blossoming on the narrow roof. A small shrub had shot up past the chimney, and a crown of green leaves rose along the ledge. From time to time a pair of birds would fly in from beyond the cemetery to the east, circle over the roof, and disappear again over the bare fields.

Since the tragedy with Chaim Vidaver and Anton Kraft, Gitele had sunk into despair. Her sense of powerlessness had become unbearable, and she became more and more isolated from everything around her. So many of the threats that once seemed distant and unreal—a summons from the Gestapo, deportation, death itself—all of these now seemed inevitable. For days on end, she had walked around in a panic, unable to look Vigdor in the eye. As for Vigdor, he seemed utterly changed since his return from the Gestapo. For weeks now he'd been brooding in silence, refusing to touch the watery soup that was delivered each day. He wanted nothing more than to die. Sometimes he uttered strange words to Gitele, the disjointed sentences of someone who'd surrendered his will to live. His eyes were swollen and bloodshot from the Gestapo's blows, and his gaze was cold and distant, like a man possessed. Everything that had taken place between him and Gitele two months before had floated away like a branch rent from a tree in a storm and carried off into a whirlwind. They were strangers to each other, cut off from a beautiful dream that now seemed to have lasted no more than an instant. Everything was irredeemably lost. They had become like bloodless shadows roaming the ghetto amid thousands of starving Jewish ghosts.

Things had taken a turn for the worse when, not long after Zelda died, a couple from Konin came to live with Gitele. They came with a bundle of clothes tied to a stick and an infant hidden in a handwoven basket. The moment they arrived, the mother had ominous words for Gitele: "If, God forbid, they catch the two of us—if that happens, please, Gitele, be a mother to our little child. He doesn't breastfeed anymore. All he needs is a little warm water with sugar. He's really a little angel. Never cries, sleeps all day. And when he opens his little eyes . . ."

Then she suddenly threw her arms around Gitele's delicate body and burst into tears.

When the couple from Konin first arrived with their baby, Gitele felt a warm glow in her heart, driving the darkness away like Shabbos candles illuminating the night. Whenever they caressed their child, Gitele felt overcome with obscure impulses bordering on madness. When she was alone in the room, she would run her hands over her body, and, closing her eyes, she would touch her tiny, barely formed breasts. They were cold beneath the tips of her fingers. When she squeezed slightly, a blue vein would appear on the white skin, linked to a system of faint, jagged roots.

And then, without warning, disaster struck.

The couple left the apartment for a brief interval, leaving the baby in his basket. As they made their way through the ghetto streets, they were caught in a roundup, along with a group of other Jews—and they never returned.

From that day on, the baby belonged to Gitele—to Gitele and her diaphanous body. By a sinister twist of fate, Gitele was now the baby's mother. She was convinced that her own dark thoughts were responsible for taking his parents away. Now, for days on end, the infant's tortured chirping was the only sound in the room. And then a crazy idea occurred to Gitele: she would breastfeed the child herself.

Overcome with terror, as if she were standing before God, she uncovered her breast and lifted the tiny boy. Feeling the warmth of Gitele's skin, he became still and placed his mouth over her dry nipple. Gitele closed her eyes and then a sharp pain seized her, almost making her stumble. The baby had bitten her nipple, then, flailing his little hands in the air, had scratched Gitele's breast. Overcome with shame, Gitele laid the infant on her lap and sat up on the cot, staring into the empty room. Tears fell from her eyes, dripping slowly onto her bare chest and sliding all the way down her body until they fell on the infant's head and finally moistened his hungry blue lips.

✦

Around midnight, they began boiling the bones in the black barrels in the kitchen shed. The smell wafted through the windows and floated through the alleyways. Countless shadowy figures clutching empty bowls pressed into the dark corridors leading to the kitchen. A crowd also assembled behind the closed gate to the courtyard, waiting with bowed heads like a gathering of ghosts with long faces. The glare of rabid hunger shone in their eyes like glowworms. Huddling under a low roof jutting into the alley, they kept their eyes fixed on the steam rising from the chimney over the kitchen shed. It was not ordinary steam. It had a rosy hue and hovered for a long time over the rooftops like a heavy raincloud, then dissipated and made its way into the houses around the courtyard through cracks in the windows. It drifted through the vacant hallways and even into the cellars. People living in the alleyways had waited all day for the Bat to cook the bones; once the water boiled down, there would be a tasty broth with tiny shreds of meat. Now the broth was being distributed among the crowd. Who knew when they'd next have bones to boil?

Vigdor surprised the onlookers with what he did next. After ladling out the broth, he began without warning to toss the dry, deathly white bones out of the window into the darkness of the yard. He remained hidden inside the kitchen shed, like an invisible God hurling lightning down to the world below. The bones scattered in the courtyard, falling on outstretched arms and into black pots. They struck people on their heads, on their chests, and across their faces. And, finally, a tangle of hands reached down to pick them up, clutching them tightly as if pressing the dead bones of a beloved for the last time.

17

The Decree

Ominous reports began circulating through the ghetto, and before long they all turned out to be true. In the middle of the night, as the Bat kept his strange vigil, he would climb onto a roof near Gitele's room. He would dart about on the sloping boards like the shadow of a cloud blown by a storm. Then he would creep in through the window and stand before Gitele like a sorcerer who had materialized from another world. She would be lying on the wooden cot with the baby, awaiting Vigdor's nightly visit. For some time now, the baby had been in the habit of soothing himself at night by suckling at Gitele's small breasts. Her nipples grew tender, and the sleepy baby would latch on for hours. Gitele was astonished to find that, as if in answer to her prayers, a pale, sweet liquid began to flow from her breasts—though she could not be sure if it was milk or teardrops that she had never wiped away.

Soon the Germans gave orders to close down the soup kitchens, surrender the big pots, and disassemble the brick stoves. Now that Vigdor could no longer stay in the kitchen shed, he settled permanently in Gitele's room. The only thing he brought along was a large, empty birdcage, which he set on the roof.

Meanwhile spring had arrived, bathing the low roofs of the ghetto in a gentle haze. Sometimes a warm wind blew through the courtyards like the flutter of a Turkish shawl. Somewhere beyond the fenced-in lots and crooked alleyways, wheat was sprouting in the Polish fields. The air was permeated by the sweet smell of red poppies and the ripening leaves of beet plants. A soft blue light shimmered in the alleyways. Ever since Vigdor had moved in with Gitele, a chorus of birds could be heard overhead. A happy family of birds had built a nest between the weeds sprouting from the corners of the roof. Barn swallows and sparrows would come by to visit, scuttling around the eaves before setting off again. And in the midst of it all, a solitary songbird had decided to make its home in the birdcage the Bat had set on the roof. Neither he nor Gitele could tell what species it belonged to. It had pointed, blue-gray, velvety wings, and its brown eyes glistened like a dove's. But Vigdor could recognize a dove in an instant, and this was no dove. It had long legs and a flexible neck covered with sparse, pale feathers. When it opened its beak, a broken trill resounded through the alleyway like the sound of scattering coins. It must have been attracted by the green grass sprouting on the roof. This was astonishing because, except for the few birds that gathered around Gitele's roof, most birds stayed away from the ghetto. The Jews hardly saw swallows, pigeons, sparrows, or starlings, unless it was during a funeral procession along the ghetto's northern end. Whenever a corpse was buried, the birds always gathered in noisy throngs. They would assemble along the barbed-wire fence near the cemetery, singing to the vacant sky. At these times, it seemed as if magical violins were hiding behind the bushes just beyond the fence. These birds came in swarms from the Łagiewniki Forest and the nearby orchards, which were already in bloom. Zigzagging through the air, they flew over the dark alleys leading to fields where the Jews buried their dead.

The mysterious bird that had moved into the cage on the roof must have also come from the open fields beyond the graveyard. Gitele and Vigdor watched it with amazement. At times its face looked almost human. When its eyes fluttered, Gitele imagined she could see Zelda peering out. The bird would make a sharp warbling sound that ended in a cough, just as Zelda had done before she died. And it kept its eyes half closed, watching the world through a narrow crack—just like Zelda had. It must have been her sister's soul, taking possession of this strange winged creature to watch over Gitele, to ensure she was taking care of the orphan the couple from Konin had left behind. They moved the cage into their room so they could be reminded of the bird's presence even in the depths of night.

Ever since the bird's arrival, other birds would visit Gitele in her dreams almost every night. They arrived in great flocks and circled around her cot. Gitele felt herself rising from her wooden bed, floating weightlessly out the window and over vast fields, supported by wings that took the place of her arms. Black lines of birds stretched out before and behind her, and the whole sky echoed with the flutter of wings. In her dreams, she could distinguish every species of bird: the tiny field birds in front of her, the swallows, canaries, bullfinches, and starlings behind—and finally, at the rear, a string of eagles and other birds of prey. Gray-and-white seagulls flew beneath her, gazing over the sea and diving from time to time, catching fish that leapt from the waves. In her dream, when Gitele was surrounded by birds on all sides, a sweet song would burst forth effortlessly from her throat, merging with the whoosh of the wind. She saw herself reflected in the birds' eyes. Her face was clear and radiant, healed of the smallpox scars, and she flew through the clouds with the same grace and lightness as the birds. But then, in the middle of her dream, a feeling of shame came over her; all these birds were there only for her, but the sky was *too* crowded with them. Suddenly, everything fell silent. Then the silence was shattered by the voice of the woman from Konin. There she was, walking arm in arm with her husband, approaching the edge of a field in the dim light of the setting sun. They looked like two birds swooping into an abyss. A blinding light shone from their faces, and Gitele had to turn away. She wanted to tell them something, but they disappeared in the flickering light of the setting sun. The last remaining lights from the stars flashed at odd intervals, and, finally, darkness engulfed the earth.

✦

And then one day, without warning, an ominous sign: the sound of the birds on the roof ceased, all at once. No one noticed that they had all flown off to the eastern fields beyond the ghetto. Though many weeks of summer still remained, the grass on the roof suddenly dried up, turning a sickly, ashen color. The green-colored rotting slats on the roof began to show through.

A naked, thousand-eyed specter seemed to be standing in the middle of the room. It was the specter of hunger. Gitele and the infant tried to hide from its penetrating gaze. Tiny white pockets began to appear beneath their eyes, like quivering rose petals. Who knows what would have happened if it hadn't been for Vigdor? Every day she awaited him anxiously. And Gitele wasn't the only one depending on him. All the women from the kitchen shed would watch for him, peering out at the street through cracks in the windows. Concealed under their kerchiefs, they clutched small bowls, glasses, and even silver-plated Shabbos cups they'd still managed to hold onto.

Vigdor was lurking among the gravestones in the cemetery, keeping an eye on the bird nets he'd set up. He knew he was committing an unforgivable crime against the sleek gray creatures flying overhead with such joy. But he couldn't stop thinking about Gitele and the baby and the women holding their Shabbos cups out to him. Two sparrows were already lying in one of the nets, their tiny necks caught in the webbing. He was hoping to trap some of the larger wild birds as well. He had the black pot ready, resting on a pile of branches and twigs. Soon the steam would be rising off the boiling water. By nightfall, Gitele and the baby would have warm soup made from the bird meat, and the women, a few spoonfuls of broth for their Shabbos cups.

✦

Everyone anticipated what would happen next. At night, shadowy crowds of Germans were gathering behind the fences along the alleyways, near the chapel. At the slightest unfamiliar sound from the other side, Jews took refuge in concealed rooms, in attics, in basements. Vigdor hid along with Gitele and the baby in the attic room. Then suddenly it became silent.

One morning at dawn, a timid ghetto sun ascended the sky, surveying the silent city like a cracked mirror. A greenish glow settled over the alleyways. At times the sun seemed to freeze in the sky, as if refusing to complete its ascent. A broken shadow fell upon the earth.

It was silent in the room. The bird was dozing in its cage, its pupils rolling back and forth in the orbits of its eyes. It must have been lost in some distant bird-dream. Gitele had already risen to prepare the pot for Vigdor. This morning, she felt a strange new feeling, as if a miracle of nature were occurring within her body. Her tiny nipples had begun to swell, and drop after drop had fallen into the baby's mouth. She felt an odd combination of fear and joy, the shock of the unfamiliar combined with the greatest happiness she had ever known. She gazed long and hard at Vigdor, then at the baby. She wanted to cry, but instead of tears a smile momentarily lit up her face. As she handed the pot to Vigdor, she spoke a few clipped words: "Soon, Vigdor. Soon, I'll be feeding yours too, your child. It will be just after the end of summer."

Vigdor held his breath and stared at her. Even the smallpox spots on her face radiated light. But when he extended his hand toward her to caress her, he was interrupted by the sound of inhuman screams from the courtyard below.

Gitele grabbed the baby and ran to the hiding place they'd constructed under the eaves. Vigdor turned to look at the bird, whose gaze was frantically darting around the room, while rays of sunlight reflected off its brown and gold pupils. It flapped its wings against the sides of the cage, a splintering cackle echoing from its narrow beak.

It would be dangerous to leave the bird in the room. But to bring it into the hiding place would have been even worse. Vigdor hesitated, unsure what to do. Deranged screams rose from the courtyard below—a woman crying out in a high, piercing voice. It sounded like a blade had been hurled through the blue sky into a human body. Finally, Vigdor grabbed the bird and rushed to the window. He let it go and watched as it stretched out its wings and flew around in circles over the rooftop. Finally it disappeared behind the low-lying clouds.

Only then did Vigdor retreat into the hiding place in the attic.

✦

It was impossible to see them from their hiding place, despite the large cracks running down the slats on the walls. But there was no mistaking the resounding rhythm of their boots, pounding the street like rolling thunder. The black shadows of the German soldiers swept up and down rickety wooden staircases. Amid their sharp, knifelike voices, a timorous Jewish lament could be heard from inside the houses. It was as if two voices were struggling with one another, flooding the silence with a torrent of sound. Suddenly a whistle cut through the air like lightning, and Jews could be heard crying out from across the courtyard. A group had been found hiding in a cellar, and the Germans were hauling them into the street.

Then silence reigned once again. Vigdor and Gitele huddled together in the corner of their hideout, listening in the dark. A finely woven spiderweb hung from the walls. The baby was resting in Gitele's lap, propped up on her pregnant belly.

Someone was climbing the wooden staircase. No, it was definitely two people. Gitele covered up the baby's head and open mouth with her shirt. Now the door to their attic room was flung open, and they could hear sharp cries of laughter coming from inside.

"Ha! Ha! Hoooo!"

"HAAAAAA!"

"*Du lieber Gott!* Have a look at this, Hans. A birdcage. *Eine Käfig.* Look!"

"A birdcage?"

"*Jawohl,* the Jew was keeping a bird."

"*Ach, mein Gott,* a poor little bird locked up in the ghetto!"

"Look at the floor, look at all these feathers. Must've been a songbird of some kind."

"*Na, ja.* A poor songbird in the ghetto."

"Looks like it was a goldfinch."

"No, no, *mein lieber.* I think it was just a starling. Look at the feathers."

"No, I'm sure of it. This isn't a starling. It was definitely a goldfinch—or, if not, maybe a chickadee."

"A chickadee? *Quatsch!* Ha, ha! Definitely not. Definitely not."

"Yes, I'm sure. Now that I look at it. Definitely a chickadee. Back at home they call these fat chicks. I'm sure of it. Look, it must've had a green belly and gray wings."

"No, it wasn't a chickadee and it wasn't a goldfinch. Just a plain old starling. These are the feathers. Oh, my poor little starling."

"My poor chickadee!"

✦

When they were discovered, Vigdor was the first one to come out of the hideout. Gitele followed him, together with the child. As they were led out, they noticed the birdcage had been left on the floor by the doorway. The courtyard was filled with a crowd of other Jews who'd gotten caught in the raid. They were all led down a back alleyway to the chapel on the other side of the ghetto fence. Walking behind Vigdor, Gitele carried the baby concealed in a woven basket.

Soon they arrived at a deserted square. Before them, on the other side of the open field, the church tower rose in the shadows. The golden cross jutted out from the rounded cupola like a giant red finger pointing at the sky. The Germans ordered everyone to kneel.

The earth was black and moist with rain and cold to the touch. Gitele and Vigdor were kneeling side by side. Gitele had still not uncovered the basket where the baby was hidden. A single thought filled her mind: she had to find the woman from Konin and return her baby to her. She would go up to the woman, hand her the baby, and say with infinite gentleness. "You see, I've taken care of him. I've been like a mother to him." And then she would confide her secret, that here, beneath her heart, she was carrying a child of her own. Her own child. Her very own.

As Vigdor sat kneeling on the ground, he kept his eyes fixed on the folds and notches in the earth. Countless ants were running back and forth, in and out of clumps of black soil. In and out, in and out. He bent down, grabbed a handful of dirt, and squeezed it slowly. Ants fell to the ground in a mad scramble, eluding their fierce enemy. Some of the ants remained in Vigdor's hand, scurrying around as if to find something in the folds of his palm.

Then the sky grew darker. Massive gray rain clouds were approaching, blowing in from the north. A warm summer rain began to fall. As the heavens darkened over the kneeling Jews, the sun could still be seen in the eastern part of the sky, shining in an oasis of blue. Suddenly, the parting clouds revealed an immense rainbow. Everyone raised their faces to the sky in a single motion. The rainbow was cracked down the middle and streaks of color were dancing around the edges in a wild tumult of light. Magnificent rays of sunlight lit up the sky and shone over the earth where the Jews were kneeling. They were encircled by red flames of light as if a fire had just been kindled.

Vigdor was still clutching his handful of dirt, watching the ants in their mad scramble. Then, slipping through the assembled group of kneeling Jews, the cat from the soup kitchen suddenly emerged and came to rest at Vigdor's feet. Vigdor craned his neck behind him and surveyed the crowd. Everyone from his alleyway was there, kneeling behind him. The women from the kitchen shed were all there. Their faces looked sunken and dead, and their bones stuck out under black kerchiefs and shawls. He closed his eyes for a moment, and in his mind's eye he saw the white bones he'd thrown to them from the soup kitchen window. It seemed as if he was himself now kneeling amid a heap of white bones.

Meanwhile, still on her knees, Gitele uncovered the baby's head and began to nurse him. Tears came from Gitele's eyes, but she did not make a sound. Vigdor turned and watched as the big, round teardrops slid down her cheek and merged with the raindrops falling on the baby's head. Vigdor thought he could see the colors of the rainbow reflected in Gitele's eyes. As he turned his gaze upward, a flock of black birds approached from the east and circled, high in the sky, just above the assembly of kneeling Jews. Then they set off again, flying toward the fading glimmer of the rainbow. As Vigdor watched, the birds disappeared into the white glare of the sun, which was suspended in the blue, serene ocean of the sky.

18

Flames from the Earth

The night after the raid when Vigdor, Gitele, and the others were taken, a group of shadowy figures darted through the ghetto streets. They ran up and down the rickety, wooden staircases and searched through empty apartments. They rummaged feverishly among abandoned objects, tearing through old bedding and clothes. Wielding sharp axes, they chopped through beds and cupboards, and smashed floors and walls. The shadows flitted from room to room, from courtyard to courtyard, crisscrossing an entire section of the ghetto, now emptied of Jews. They went into cellars and climbed into attics, occasionally finding an old pot or pan, even digging around in the ashes of stoves that hadn't been lit for many days.

These desperate people were not from outside. They came from the eastern section of the ghetto, which dozed on in the ghostly night. They wore pointed hats with yellow stars stitched on them, leather jackets, and tall boots. Their faces looked calm, and they bore few signs of hunger as they carried out their solemn task. Their shadowy hands were propelled by a demonic force that seemed to divide them from the Jewish people. They searched with great efficiency through the dark corners of rooms now devoid of Jews, as if they themselves had once lived there. They ran in pairs or groups of three, never alone. Some rummaged through hay sacks, others flipped madly through the pages of sacred tomes. Once a cry suddenly rang out: on a sunken cot, beside a table with a prayer book, someone had found a human body. The man appeared to be asleep. They shook him by the shoulders to rouse him, but his face remained unmoved, as if sealed with wax. A faint smile wrinkled the edges of his mouth, giving him a peaceful look. When his eyes refused to open, they covered his face and fled.

Sometimes, as they searched an attic room they would come upon a hanged man, still dangling from the rope. The body would usually be completely naked. It would hardly look human, the ribs twisted and the spine flattened like a pane of glass. These were the bodies of men who had long ago conquered their fear of death. They had resolved to meet it head on, leaving behind their hollow bodies and bloodless veins.

Meanwhile, people began hurling abandoned objects out of windows, and in the streets in front of each house, there were mounting heaps of clothing, furniture, books, and sacred tomes. Others came to sort through the objects. Some of the bedsheets, kitchen utensils, and furniture would be shipped off in trucks to the Germans in town. Things deemed useless would be placed into separate piles and consigned to flames.

Soon smoke began rising from broken pieces of wood, old clothes, and the fanned-out pages of books, soiling the gray light of the dawn. The quickest to burn were the pages of holy books. Prayer books trembled with fear as the flames devoured them, while little volumes of the Psalms and great, proud volumes of scripture refused to open their sacred pages to the spreading fire. They huddled together for safety, but little by little the foul-smelling, deadly smoke enveloped them. Even then, the sacred pages clung desperately to each other as the flames engulfed them. Sparks rose from the conflagration like flaming red letters inscribed on the darkened sky. Then the sparks fell backward and arched in the sky before disappearing into the rising cloud of smoke. From a distance they looked like stars tumbling from the depths of heaven.

As the black flames rose higher and higher above the charred remains of Jewish lives, the gray ash of burnt books collected around the base of the heap like a fallen crown. When nothing was left to burn, the sparks abandoned their mad dance, and the flames turned back toward the earth to lick the ashes. In the eastern sky, the sun appeared behind heavy clouds. The colorless rays of dawn fell on dying embers.

✦

And now sepulchres of red brick can be seen standing over sunken tombs. For several days, no one has come to bury their dead. The darkening hours of twilight pass unheeded. Has death suddenly given up? Why such deep silence over the graves? As you move through the alleyways of the ghetto, the darkness becomes palpable. A timorous voice pierces the night silence. Could there be a child here somewhere, crying in the gloom?

To the east, beyond the ghetto bridge, a blue-tinged cloud floats by, almost flush with the ground. Has it fallen from the sky? Could it be a wandering supplicant seeking entrance to the ghetto? No, it's no cloud, but smoke from a rolling fire heading toward the ghetto bridge. A sharp wind blows in from the eastern fields, and now the wooden beams holding the barbed wire begin to burn. Soon flames will engulf the railings and the stairs. For now, it's still breathing: the last, unhurried breaths of the battered, deserted bridge.

Someone violently unlatches a window and shoves it open. A high youthful voice cries out in Yiddish, piercing the sky like a sharp blade. The fire is spreading—soon the last remaining windows, roofs, sheds, and cellars will be burning. For the time being, the bridge is still shrouded in silence. The child has stopped screaming, and the western sky glows with flames circling over the bridge. They ascend into the sky, mingling with the wavering dust of the Milky Way. The flames are gradually veiled by distant clouds; then they disappear in the darkness like drowning men.

✦

As dusk descends upon the countryside, the drowsy sun glimmers over bare potato fields beyond the ghetto fence. A thick blanket of fog envelops the tops of the pine trees in the Łagiewniki Forest. Although it is late summer, the exhalation of the earth is already cold and frosty. Across the vast open fields, the shoots of the potato plants hesitantly poke through cracks in the earth. In a clearing of plowed land, behind the Kaczmarek Inn, a goat is grazing in the twilight. Its lean flanks are covered with black spots. Although there's little trace of new growth to be seen, the goat has found tiny dry roots in the fissures and folds of the ground. Nearby, a barefoot boy in a torn shirt with long sleeves is lying in the field, holding the goat by a rope. Try as it might to set off on its own, the goat can't break free from the boy's grasp. Now the boy props himself up on his elbows and surveys the wide, empty expanse all around him.

The Kaczmarek Inn has been closed for weeks, its windows boarded shut. Apart from the boy and his goat, there's no sign of life for miles around. The synagogue that was left outside the confines of the ghetto is gone, leaving only its charred walls as a reminder. After a while, the boy stands up and tugs at the goat, but the animal refuses to leave its spot beside the dead roots in the potato beds. The boy bends down and picks up a handful of twigs, which he presses into cigarette papers and lights with a match. After a long time, a tiny blue flame appears and the black smoke circles overhead.

The goat turns away from the smoke and closes its eyes. Then the boy bends down and caresses the goat's muzzle.

"Poor Jewish goat. You're so silly, so unlucky. But you're much luckier than your old owners, the ones who used to live over there."

Hearing a human voice, the goat turns toward the boy and gives him a long, melancholy gaze. Then it grows suspicious, and the boy is suddenly startled by the dark Jewish look in its round black eyes, framed by thick white lashes. The boy squeezes the rope tighter.

Again the goat bends to the earth, resuming its grazing among the dry roots. Again the peasant boy blows on the tip of his cigarette of twigs and leaves. Sparks burst forth with a hissing sound. As twilight darkens the sky, the boy can no longer see anything around him, not even his bare feet. The only light comes from the tiny flame glowing at the end of his stick. The boy and his goat are together in the glow of burning embers. Night has fallen and stars flicker in the lonely sky. Darkness descends from the sky as the earth greedily devours the last remaining traces of day. And when everything is bathed in utter blackness and the earth and sky have merged, the sparks burst forth again, rising upward like a bridge of light, ascending from the earth. The celestial ocean begins to glow, and the frozen stars look down in shame. The flames from the earth dance wildly and will not go out.

1943–1954

TRANSLATOR'S AFTERWORD

My only desire was to see the eternal within the evanescent,
the symbolic within the passing show.
—Isaiah Spiegel (1973)

From the moment he returned to his native city of Łódź at the end of World War II, Isaiah Spiegel was consumed with the problem of how to use the resources of literary art to describe the colossal trauma we now call the Holocaust. As he put it in 1949, "Writers of literature, among Jews and other nations, will be searching for a long time for the proper form with which to express artistically the drama the Jews have recently endured."[1] Yiddish writers published numerous diaries, memoirs, poems, and works of reportage about the Nazi nightmare in the immediate aftermath of the war, but they have produced precious few *Holocaust novels*, if by "Holocaust novel" we mean an extended narrative including imagined scenes and events and focusing on the ghetto or camp experience. A novel had been written in Yiddish in the early years of the war by Warsaw Ghetto inmate Zalmen Skalov. Preserved in Emanuel Ringelblum's Oyneg Shabes archives and published in 1954 as *Der haknkrayts* (The Swastika), this novel was written before the Jews' ultimate fate was clearly understood, and Skalov was murdered too soon to learn the truth about the Final Solution. In the 1950s, Rakhmiel Bryks wrote a pair of novellas about the Łódź Ghetto, and K. Tzetnik (pen name of Yehiel De-Nur) serialized a trilogy of novels about the Holocaust, the most famous of which was his highly graphic inside view of Auschwitz, *Dos hoyz fun di lyalkes* (House of Dolls).[2] But it was not until 1966, when Spiegel wrote *Flames from the Earth*, subtitling it "*roman*" (A Novel), that the first fully fledged Yiddish novel focusing on the ghetto was published in the postwar period. Here was an extended narrative with a diverse cast of characters whose fates interconnect in surprising ways in and around the Łódź Ghetto, written by a Yiddish author who had survived nearly five years in the Nazi death machine.

The challenge of shaping a novel around the ghetto experience can hardly be overestimated. For one thing, the reality of life in what was in essence an open-air prison, where individual agency was dramatically curtailed and violent death came to seem inevitable, would seem to defy the basic requirements for a novel. How could an author create the kinds of turning points, based on individual choice and self-assertion, that are integral to the novel form and indispensable for creating suspense? Moreover, some survivors were so determined to preserve a rigorously accurate record of the war years that they may not have immediately recognized the value of a Holocaust work containing embellished or fictionalized events. For these reasons, it was often taken for granted that unadorned documentation, not novelistic re-creation, was the order of the day. Seen in this context, Spiegel's work must be seen as a bold assertion that, indeed, even the unprecedented trauma of the Holocaust could and *should* be framed by the novelist's imagination. How did Spiegel create this work, and what unique perspectives on the ghetto experience does it offer?

As noted in the introduction, Spiegel had written poems and short vignettes during the four years he was interned in the ghetto, and he used many of these manuscripts as the basis for three volumes of short stories (Ghetto Kingdom, 1945; Stars over the Ghetto, 1948; and People in the Abyss, 1949) and a volume of poetry (And There Was Light, 1949). It was only several years later, after settling in Israel, that Spiegel stepped back from the episodic nature of his story collections and, inspired by the encouragements of a literary critic, ventured the panoramic view of the ghetto that became *Flames from the Earth*. Rather than constructing the work from scratch, Spiegel turned back to his published stories as well as to what he called his *sheymes*, his personal archive of manuscripts recovered from the ghetto. He selected certain episodes from previously written material, such as the scene in which a cartload of bones is brought into the ghetto, added some entirely new scenes, and created links between episodes to weave together a cohesive narrative.[3] In its manner of composition, then, the novel can be considered a hybrid work, combining firsthand accounts of the ghetto experience, written sometimes within days of the events described, with reflections from up to twenty years later. He indicates this strategy in a note appended to the end of the novel: "Written: 1943–1954." This affirms the *authenticity* of the material, that it was written in the presence of the horrors described, while also explaining that the novel was completed at a temporal distance from the events. (It is not entirely clear why the years between 1955 and 1966 were omitted from this dating, since, as Spiegel explained in an interview, he continued to add material throughout this period.) This strategy of blending material written in the ghetto with later work suggests that Spiegel resisted relying solely on his memory to capture the emotional core of the ghetto experience. It also enables him to legitimate his work as an authoritative document of the Holocaust.

At the same time, *Flames from the Earth* differs from the genre of reportage, which had been a major prose form during the war. Spiegel's work is decidedly *literary*, drawing on techniques we associate with European modernism, such as interior monologue, the indirect narration of events, and a collage-like method of composition. Other modernistic features include his symbolic layering of physical settings, the cinematic use of color, the animation of inanimate objects, the emphasis on dreams and altered psychological states, and the merging of mundane reality with the world of myth. Among fellow Jewish writers, his work recalls the symbolism of the Soviet Yiddish writer Der Nister (1884–1950) and the fantastical dreamscapes of Polish Jewish writer Bruno Schulz (1892–1942). While Spiegel never loses sight of the imperative to memorialize those who were murdered, his insistently literary approach suggests that he felt that this task could not be accomplished by documentation alone. It was also necessary to call upon the range of modern literary techniques that writers in diverse linguistic traditions have developed to interpret reality and fire the imagination.

To create a sense of the unfolding of events through time, Spiegel punctuates his chapters with lyrical evocations of the changing seasons. We begin in the fourth winter of the war, when deportations to the mysterious "East" have already thinned out the ghetto population; and we end in the late summer of 1944, when the ghetto has been liquidated and all that remains are abandoned streets and courtyards. But this inexorable march toward death is framed by passages evoking the cycles of the natural world: we move from a "snowy wasteland," where the winds spread "thin white sheets along the windowsills like delicate death shrouds" to the fields of summer, where "the shoots of the potato plants hesitantly poke through cracks in the earth." The changing seasons closely link the chronology of the novel with the final stages of the Łódź Ghetto (the period from January to August of 1944), while also functioning symbolically to counteract the theme of violent death, which remains clearly in view throughout. At many points in the novel, the anticipation of spring is felt acutely by everyone in the ghetto, especially Gitele, whose pregnancy and dreams for the future appear to be confirmed by the cycles of nature. A powerful contrast is thus established between the inexorability of the Nazi death machine on the one hand and the irrepressible cycles of nature on the other.

The natural world is also evoked throughout the novel with the constant presence of real and symbolic birds. Birds play multiple roles in the text: they are the target of the Nazi Jessicke's sadistic shooting sprees; they also become an indispensable source of food for the Jews in the ghetto. They symbolize at once freedom and fragility, a portent of hope and a sign of otherworldly mystery. Jessicke sees in a raven the "black spirit of the ghetto Jews," while the saintly bell ringer seems to become a bird himself at the moment before his execution: "From far away, he looked like a bird swaying backward on spindly legs, waiting to take flight. Soon the bird would spread his huge tremulous wings and soar off on a distant journey to a long, peaceful, shadowy sleep." Tellingly, Vigdor and Gitele keep in their room a surprisingly companionable bird that resembles a dove but resists any sort of clear classification. They release the bird just before they are captured, and from their hiding place they listen as the German soldiers try in vain to identify the bird by its few remaining feathers. The bird has survived the Nazi raid, but we are left wondering if it is part of the natural world at all. Has the bird, like the Jews in the ghetto, disappeared into the intangible realm of memory and dream?

Another key to the novel's power is Spiegel's use of multiple perspectives. Using the technique of internal monologue, Spiegel lays bare the subjective experiences of a diverse set of characters, who inhabit radically different positions in the Nazi universe. The primary characters are Vigdor and Gitele (lovers who are active in the Jewish resistance movement), Antoni (a Polish peasant who is drawn into the drama of Jewish suffering against his will), Nikodem (a benevolent Polish bell ringer who lives in a church near the periphery of the ghetto), Stefan Kaczmarek (a Polish tavern keeper who betrays Nikodem to preserve his smuggling business), and Franz Jessicke (a Nazi guard who blackmails local Poles for personal gain). Secondary characters include Anton Kraft (a virtuoso violinist brought to the ghetto from Prague) and Chaim Vidaver (the charismatic leader of the ghetto resistance, who struggles to uphold morale among his fellow Jews). By inhabiting the points of view of these disparate characters, Jewish and non-Jewish, the novel creates a kaleidoscopic image of the ghetto universe as a complex, interlocking web of relationships structured by radically uneven hierarchies of power. Unlike the highly compressed stories Spiegel had been publishing for two decades, *Flames from the Earth* invites readers to consider the wide-reaching scope of the Holocaust, while illuminating how multiple parties—Jews, Poles, and even Nazis—were all entangled in a single, unfathomable tragedy.

At the same time that it blends wartime and postwar writings, *Flames from the Earth* combines historical and invented material. Spiegel often describes characters he knew personally and events he observed in the ghetto, while also inserting wholly imaginary elements to bring out the allegorical potential in his material. A case in point is chapter 3, "The Dead Stradivarius," where we meet the Czech violinist Anton Kraft (Spiegel uses his actual name). Kraft was one of a handful of virtuoso musicians in the ghetto. He had been a member of the Prague Philharmonic until 1939, when Jews were prohibited from attending theaters and concerts.[4] In 1941, he was deported to the Łódź Ghetto, where he entertained his fellow residents in private circles, until January 17, 1944, when Chaim Rumkowski issued a decree requiring all musical instruments to be surrendered. In what was yet another in a series of mounting humiliations, Kraft's genius was suppressed, and the ghetto Jews were deprived of the consolation of music. As Oskar Rosenfeld noted in his diary, "Beethoven, Mozart, Chopin, Schumann [fell] silent in the ghetto forever . . . To the torments of hunger and cold [were] added the unappeased craving for music."[5] *Flames from the Earth* contains a scene in which Kraft recovers a violin hidden in Zelda's room (quite possibly a scene invented by Spiegel), before playing a dramatic requiem as she expires. Blending fact and fiction (or poetically embellishing what may have been an actual event), Spiegel creates an allegory for Jewish courage, perseverance, and mutual support.

Spiegel also places at the center of his novel difficult issues historians of the Łódź Ghetto have grappled with, above all the question of resistance—or lack thereof. In Warsaw, Sobibór, Częstochowa, Białystok, and a number of smaller ghettos in the eastern territories, Jews managed to organize movements of armed resistance, typically during the final liquidation phase of the ghettos. Although these uprisings met with little material success, they were essential for morale, and they have figured centrally in Jewish cultural memory. The day set aside to commemorate the Holocaust, Yom Ha-Shoah, roughly coincides with the anniversary of the Warsaw Ghetto uprising. And Hirsh Glik's song for the Vilna Ghetto resistance fighters, "Zog nit keynmol" (Never Say), has become one of the most widely sung anthems at Holocaust commemoration events.[6] The Łódź Ghetto, however, is typically remembered as a place where resistance was impossible. The Holocaust historian Isaiah Trunk concludes his monumental history of the Łódź Ghetto by listing factors that mitigated against any concerted resistance, ranging from the thorough Germanification of the rest of the city (which isolated the ghetto from any potential allies) to false hopes raised by misinformation about the fate of the deportees and the imminence of the war's end. Above all, Trunk emphasizes the demoralization of the Jews: "The Nazi annihilation strategy toward the Jewish population was that, after the victims would be sufficiently 'processed' for a lengthy time through hunger, terror, and complete isolation from the outside, they would be powerless and allow anything to be done with them that would be demanded of them."[7]

Seen in this context, Spiegel's decision to focus his narrative around a resistance group suggests a desire to rectify the historical record—or at least to restore the dignity of Jews he lived and suffered alongside in the ghetto. He may indeed be tacitly responding to Trunk, whose history first appeared in Yiddish in 1962 and whom Spiegel knew from Łódź before the war. The group that Vigdor meets in Zelda's room (chapter 3) and later visits in the cellar (chapter 9) is modeled on an actual group whose activities centered on clandestine radio listening. This was a group of Jews from diverse backgrounds, including a Zionist, a Gerer Hasid, a member of the Polish Socialist Party, and a Bundist, who were in possession of a homemade radio (radios were forbidden to Jews and Poles by a decree of December 1939). Spiegel's own brother and one of his brothers-in-law participated directly in their activities. Members of the radio underground (referred to in Yiddish as the *radio-herers*, the "radio-hearers") risked their lives to gain information about the progress of the war. In a testimony given by the son of one ghetto resident, we learn that "[the radio] was listened to in order to keep abreast of the situation on the front and the progress of the Red Army. They knew that as soon as the Red Army approached, the Germans would liquidate the ghetto and flee westward. When they heard in the winter of 1943 to 1944 that the river froze, they immediately spread the word, and all of them went into hiding places they had prepared in the ghetto. Thus several dozen Jews were saved in the ghetto."[8] Eventually, a Jewish informer told the Nazi Criminal Police (the Kripo) about the radio-hearers, and in June of 1944, nearly all were arrested (Trunk, 398). The story of the radio-hearers forms the basis of the novel *Jacob the Liar* (1969), written by the East German Jewish writer Jurek Becker and made into two separate movies, one in East Germany (1974), the other in the United States (1999).

So too does this group figure centrally in *Flames from the Earth*. Gitele and Vigdor are among those entrusted with the task of spreading news picked up from the radio, and, while the details of the plot remain shadowy, the unnamed Jew who is hidden in the church also appears to be connected to the group. Also, the character of Chaim Vidaver, who engages in the debate in a candlelit cellar, is based on one of the central figures in the radio underground, Chaim Widawski, who was a friend of Spiegel's in the ghetto. The historical

Widawski, a member of the centrist General Zionist Party, managed to escape the Kripo roundup when the radio underground was betrayed. But, as he confronted the inevitability of his arrest and torture, he committed suicide by swallowing cyanide.[9] Spiegel incorporates the story of Widawski's suicide into his novel as one of the fragmentary tales exchanged among the women rummaging through the pile of potato skins in chapter 15. The Nazi crackdown on the movement and Widawski/Vidaver's suicide are referenced by the women, but not developed into fully fledged scenes. Like other events in the novel, these stories circulate as vague reports, pointing to the ominous fate awaiting the ghetto as a whole.

The scene where the fate of the radio-hearers is disclosed exemplifies Spiegel's technique of indirect narration, whereby key events are relayed through rumors or truncated exchanges (another example is Vigdor's account to Gitele of the death of his wife and daughter in chapter 4). This modernist technique (consider Virginia Woolf's parenthetical mention of Mrs. Ramsay's death in *To the Lighthouse*) shifts the reader's attention away from specific events and toward their larger and multiple effects.[10] It also underscores the limitations of human understanding itself and the inherently fragmentary forms in which knowledge about the world comes to us. In Spiegel's case, this narrative technique enables him to register traumatic events without allowing them to overwhelm or displace the broader, symbolic meanings he hopes to convey. Speaking about his writing in general, Spiegel explained that "I note the actual facts, but they are mainly a springboard, so to speak, for my own dreams and literary goals; I never wanted to give raw naturalism, which is properly speaking the role of documentation [and not of the novel]."[11] And so Spiegel incorporates the radio underground into the narrative less in the service of historical documentation than to create an allegory about Jewish determination and courage in the face of evil.

The central theme woven throughout the novel concerns the Jews' enduring loyalty to one another even at a time of unimaginable suffering. When we first meet Vigdor, he is in a state of psychic and emotional isolation, having lost the capacity to regard his fellow ghetto Jews as a source of support. After a chance meeting with Gitele, his former lover's sister, he enters the warm embrace of a group of idealistic Jews determined to fight for their freedom. Just as Vigdor's physical passion is rekindled by this encounter, so too does he recognize that a future beyond death and misery may be possible by collective action and mutual support. He feels as if he has "returned to the land of the living, where prayers ascended into the heavens like sprouting seeds yearning for the light."

Despite the religious language in this passage, the overall outlook of the novel can be described as secular. Vigdor is and remains largely alienated from traditional Judaism. He says Kaddish for the dead Jew he discovers and buries, but the words are "barely remembered" and uttered out of respect more than piety. Vigdor's focus—and Spiegel's more generally—is not on theology but on questions about moral responsibility and human solidarity. Unlike Zvi Kolitz, whose "Yosl Rakover Speaks to God" presents a Job-like figure impugning God for His failure to protect His people in the Warsaw Ghetto, Spiegel asks how human beings can continue to support one another under conditions of extreme duress. At various points in the novel, we hear cries of protest hurled at the outside world. "Why did the world refuse to help?" Vigdor asks himself. "How could everyone on the other side go on with their work? . . . Why did they celebrate their holidays? Why? Why?" But Spiegel also introduces non-Jewish characters who come to the aid of the Jews. Indeed, Vigdor's movement from isolation to fellowship is paralleled by the movement of the unnamed Jewish resistance fighter who is taken in and protected by the old bell ringer. Importantly, the bell ringer is motivated not only by his deep piety as a Roman Catholic, but also by loyalty to his son, a Polish partisan who has sent a letter to his father through the Jewish fugitive. In this case, intergenerational bonds have remained intact, just like the bonds connecting the Jewish resistance group that Vigdor joins.

Instructively the sections involving the Polish bell ringer and his execution seem to be pure invention. Not only is there no historical record of this event, but there does not appear to have been a Church of Saint Francis within view of the ghetto, as Spiegel suggests. A prewar guide indicates that such a church existed along the southern outskirts of the city, but this would have been a long way from the ghetto. Spiegel's imaginative relocation of this church and the creation of the elderly bell ringer enable him to valorize one specific element of Polish society, the old Catholic church, with its folk traditions and profound religious faith. Indeed, the scene of Nikodem's execution is without a doubt one of the most powerful of the novel. The reader's focus merges with that of the local Poles who are ordered to appear at the church to observe a hanging. All expect the victim to be another Jew caught trying to escape the ghetto. When it turns out to be the old bell ringer, they shudder in horror, recognizing something the reader has known all along: that evil knows no distinctions, that moral goodness is everywhere under assault. (Of course, not all the Catholics in the novel are heroized in this way. The villainous Stefan Kaczmarek serves as the counterpoint to Nikodem, and through Stefan's internal monologue we see how his virulent antisemitism is rooted in and justified by his understanding of his faith.)

Yet another invented episode—one of the most fanciful passages in the novel—concerns the sudden death of the Nazi guard who has blackmailed the Polish innkeeper Marta Kaczmarek into a sexual liaison. The scene leads to disaster for the forces of good, setting up the gruesome execution of the bell ringer, but it also hints at an obscure form of divine retribution. After all, the Nazi expires on the very board in the abandoned synagogue that had previously been used by Jews to purify their dead before burial. Interestingly, Spiegel also seems to be rewriting here a scene from the Babylonian Talmud. In the account of the military confrontation with Rome just preceding the destruction of the Temple, Vespasian heads off to Rome following his famous encounter with Rabban Yohanan. At this point, the new general Titus enters the Holy of Holies and has sexual intercourse with a prostitute on a Torah scroll (Gittin, 56b), paralleling Spiegel's scene in the abandoned synagogue outside the ghetto. While God in the Talmud is initially quiescent at the affront in his sacred precincts, He ultimately vanquishes Titus, humiliating him before the noblemen of Rome. By alluding to this scene, Spiegel invites readers to consider the Holocaust in relation to the mythological paradigm constructed by the rabbis in response to the destruction of the Second Temple. Jews have experienced devastation before, and they have proven equal to the challenge of cultural survival. Spiegel's novel itself may be proffered as evidence that this historical cycle is being repeated.

Spiegel's wide acceptance by his original audience suggests that his writing was well calibrated to the aesthetic tastes of postwar Yiddish readers. His poetic, impressionistic style allows for a kind of emotional outlet that evidently was—and for many may still be—deeply desired, maybe even required, for a subject as disturbing as the Holocaust. In a discussion of one of Spiegel's own literary heroes, Lord Byron, the scholar David Perkins has written that his ornate style allows for "release and expansion, a romp and revel of emotions that are ordinarily inhibited or qualified."[12] Spiegel's writing similarly encourages the release of pent-up feelings—feelings of despair, horror, rage, confusion, and loss but also deep yearnings for rebirth and for the bonds of community.

While thousands of interviews with survivors have been recorded for posterity, it is crucial to recall that survivors also used their experiences as the basis for artistically elaborated narratives. Unlike the survivor as diarist or interviewee, the survivor as novelist reminds us of other agendas beyond that of recording the empirical facts of their experiences. Novelists use their experiences to imagine extended life trajectories; they form narratives out of fragments—and reimagine the world on their own terms. In Spiegel's case, it took twenty years to construct a novel out of his Holocaust experience. To do so, he drew on diverse elements in the genre's history. *Flames from the Earth* reconfigures both the conventions of Holocaust testimony and the conventions of the realist novel, illuminating the horrors of the ghetto in the form of a compelling and entrancing work of art.

Notes

1. Yeshayahu Shpigl, *Un gevorn iz likht, lider* [And There Was Light: Poetry] (Warsaw-Łódź: Yidish-bukh, 1949), 3.

2. K. Tzetnik's work is well known today, but thanks only to the Hebrew version, which the author himself produced and which became part of the Israeli secondary school curriculum.

3. *Flames from the Earth* contains three chapters that appear in *Wind and Roots* as a single story. Chapters 15, 16, and 17 were published under the name "Beyner" [Bones].

4. Anton Kraft (1900–1944?) was a violin virtuoso and conductor, originally from Jablonec. He was connected with the FOK (Film-Opera-Koncert) Orchestra, which in its early years played mainly in the Czech programs of Prague radio. Hugh Colman, et al., *The Jews of Czechoslovakia, Historical Studies and Surveys. Vol. I.* (Philadelphia: The Jewish Publication Society of America, 1968). He was deported to the Łódź Ghetto from Prague on October 21, 1941. Kraft perished in Auschwitz.

5. Lucjan Dobroszycki, ed., *The Chronicle of the Łódź Ghetto, 1941–1944*, trans. Richard Lourie, Joachim Neugroschel, and others (New Haven, CT: Yale University Press, 1984), 434.

6. Yehiel Szeintuch, "Glik, Hirsh," in *Encyclopedia of the Holocaust: The Persecution and Murder of European Jews*, vol. 1., edited by Israel Gutman (New York: Macmillan, 1990), 544.

7. Isaiah Trunk, *Łódź Ghetto: A History*, translated and edited by Robert Moses Shapiro, introduction by Israel Gutman (Bloomington: Indiana University Press in association with the United States Holocaust Memorial Museum, 2006), 396.

8. Łódź Archives, United States Holocaust Memorial Museum: http://www.eilatgordinlevitan.com/lodz/lodz_pages/lodz_archives.html.

9. In his will, Widawski asked his movement's members to bury him in Israel, a request that was filled in 1972, when his bones were reinterred in Nahalat Yitzhak cemetery. The inscription on his tombstone reads: "He gave his life to his people and his country. He did not surrender to the enemy. His death was a symbol of the struggle against the oppressor. He was buried in the Łódź Ghetto on the 18th of Sivan, 5704. According to his will he was brought by his friends to Israel to rest forever on the 5th of Sivan, 5725. May his soul be bound up in the bond of eternal life." The municipality of Łódź erected a commemorative plaque in memory of Widawski in Podrzeczna Street. The inscription on it, written in four languages—Polish, English, Hebrew, and Yiddish—gives the following information: "On June 9, 1944, here at the side of a nonexistent house, 9 Podrzeczna st., Chaim Natatn Widawski committed suicide. He was wanted by the Gestapo for listening to a hidden radio and spreading the news to the inhabitants of Litzmannstadt Ghetto." See Gila Flam, *Singing for Survival: Songs of the Łódź Ghetto, 1940–45* (Champaign: University of Illinois Press, 1992), 178; Sarah Selver-Urbach, *Through the Window of My Home: Recollections from the Łódź Ghetto* (Jerusalem: Yad Vashem, 1986), 103; and Anna Eilenberg-

Eibeshitz, *Preserved Evidence: Ghetto Łódź* (Haifa, Israel: H. Eibeshitz Institute for Holocaust Studies, 1998), 338–40.

10. For a discussion of Woolf's narrative technique, see esp. Molly Hite, *Woolf's Ambiguities: Tonal Modernism, Narrative Strategy, Feminist Precursors* (Ithaca, NY: Cornell University Press, 2017).

11. Yechiel Szeintuch et al., *Yeshayahu Shpigel—Prozah sipurit mi-Geto Łódź* [Isaiah Spiegel—Prose Narratives from the Łódź Ghetto] (Hotsa'at sefarim 'a. sh. Y. L. Magnes, ha-Universiṭah ha-'Ivrit, 1995), 358.

12. David Perkins, *English Romantic Writers* (New York: Harcourt, Brace, and World, 1967), 784.

TRANSLATOR'S ACKNOWLEDGMENTS

My first debt of gratitude goes to Isaiah Spiegel himself, who endured unspeakable losses and kept writing. While translating his novel, I have been sustained by his faith in the power of literature to illuminate the lives and dreams of people living in extremis. I would also like to thank numerous friends and colleagues whose expertise, mentorship, and camaraderie have supported me throughout this project. I had the good fortune of participating in the Translation Fellowship Program of the Yiddish Book Center; I was also privileged to spend a year at the Frankel Center for Advanced Judaic Studies at the University of Michigan. In these fellowship programs, I benefited from the company of two inspiring cohorts of Yiddish translators and scholars. I thank the following individuals for their specific contributions at various stages of the project: Patrick Bailey, Justin Cammy, Josh Cohen, Mindl Cohen, Hannah Pollin-Galay, Zvi Gitelman, Saul Hankin, Yaakov Herskovitz, Jim Hicks, Bill Johnson, Misha Krutikov, Vivi Lachs, Benjamin Todd Lee, Nadav Linial, Deborah Dash Moore, Anita Norich, Avrom Nowershtern, Harriet Murav, Carid O'Brian, Shachar Pinsker, David Roskies, Sasha Senderovich, Jeremy Shere, Katie Silver, Nicolas Sywak, Karolina Szymaniak, Yermiyahu Aaron Taub, Miriam Udel, Jeffrey Veidlinger, and Deborah Yalen. I also thank the Frankel family—in particular Sam, Jean, Stanley, and Judy—for their generous support of Judaic studies at the University of Michigan.

Gabriel Mordoch, the Judaica librarian at the University of Michigan, assisted me by tracking down materials, including reviews of Spiegel's work and copyright information. Gordon Horwitz read the manuscript in its entirety and provided helpful insights into the history of the Łódź Ghetto. Sean Bye assisted me immeasurably with insights that only an experienced and truly wise translator can offer—about language and the meaning and scope of the art of translation.

I would also like to express my gratitude to Trevor Perri, Patrick Samuel, Faith Wilson Stein, Anne Gendler, and Anne Tappan Strother from Northwestern University Press for believing in this project and helping to shepherd it into press. Elizabeth Blachman did an outstanding job with the copyediting. I thank Michael Lenartz from the Jewish Museum in Frankfurt, who assisted me in gaining permission to use the photograph on the cover. This image was created from one of a cache of early color slides that was discovered in a shop in Vienna in 1987. The slides were made by Walter Genewein, a member of the Nazi Party who served as the chief accountant of the ghetto council. Genewein was also an amateur photographer who devoted considerable energy to documenting daily life in the ghetto. His goals as a photographer are not entirely clear, but the collection as a whole suggests he wanted to keep a record of the ghetto as a triumph of Nazi efficiency and organization. The image on the cover shows ghetto residents on a crowded, cobblestone street. Some have become aware of the photographer, and they look at him with a range of attitudes, from indifference to curiosity to defiance. This image records a moment of encounter between Jews who may not have realized they were marked for death and one of their captors.

I thank members of my family who read early drafts of the manuscript and offered much-needed suggestions and encouragement: Marianne Makman, Maynard Makman, and Judy Makman. Stephen Jacobs has embodied for me the values of commitment, perseverance, and living by one's personal vision. My mother, Eleanor Michael, not only read and commented on the manuscript, but shared her own writings with me, which have helped me understand the importance of preserving the literary legacy of the Shoah. My dear siblings—Charlotte, Ed, Gordon, and Rachel—have all inspired me in more ways than they know. I also want to express my appreciation and gratitude for my uncle Maimon Karl Maor, a fellow translator with a deep understanding of the challenges and rewards of the craft.

I would never have heard of Spiegel's novel at all if my bibliophile grandfather had not purchased a copy of it a half century ago in a used bookstore and left it unwittingly in his glorious bookshelf in Tel Aviv for me to discover many years later. I thank both my grandfather Harry Maor and grandmother Gila Maor, whose apartment at 26 Zlatapolski in north Tel Aviv housed treasures.

My children Chava, Elijah, and Jonah Makman-Levinson have touched me with their interest in Spiegel's work. My deepest gratitude goes to my wife Lisa, whose extraordinary literary sensibility I have depended on word by word (literally!), and without whose unflagging love and support I would never have undertaken this project, let alone completed it. I have been constantly mindful of the losses that both of our families suffered during the Holocaust, and I hope my work contributes to the preservation of the memory of all whose lives have been cut short by senseless brutality.

This translation is dedicated to the memory of my great-uncle Maimon Obermayer, who survived Dachau only to find that his future had become so dark that he could no longer find his way, and, like so many of his generation, he took his life just as the Nazi furnaces were being lit. Maimon sang like an angel and brought joy to all who knew him.

BOOKS BY ISAIAH SPIEGEL

Mitn ponem tsu der zun, lider [With My Face to the Sun: Poetry]. Łódź: Alfa, 1930.

Malkhes geto, noveln [Kingdom of the Ghetto: Stories]. Łódź: Dos naye lebn, 1947. English: *Ghetto Kingdom: Tales of the Łódź Ghetto*. Translated by David H. Hirsch and Roslyn Hirsch, introduction by David H. Hirsch. Evanston: Northwestern University Press, 1998.

Shtern ibern geto, noveln [Stars Over the Ghetto: Stories]. Paris: Yidishe folks-biblyotek, 1948.

Mayn leyenbukh: far fertn klas (with Shloyme Lastik) [My Textbook: For the Fourth Class]. Warsaw, 1948.

Mentshn in thom, geto-noveln [People in the Abyss: Ghetto Stories]. (Buenos Aires: IKUF, 1949).

Un gevorn iz likht, lider [And There Was Light: Poetry]. Warsaw-Łódź: Yidish-bukh, 1949.

Likht funem opgrunt, geto-noveln [Light from the Abyss: Ghetto Stories]. New York: Tsiko, 1952.

Vint un vortslen, noveln [Wind and Roots: Stories]. New York: World Jewish Culture Congress, 1955.

Di brik, noveln [The Bridge: Stories]. Tel Aviv: Perets Publ., 1963.

Flamen fun der erd, roman [Flames from the Earth: A Novel]. Tel Aviv: Yisroel-bukh, 1966.

Shtign tsum himl [Ladder to the Heavens]. Tel Aviv: Perets Publ., 1966.

Geshtaltn un profiln, literarishe eseyen [Figures and Profiles: Literary Essays], 2 vols. Tel Aviv: Hamenorah and Yisroel-bukh, 1971, 1980.

Di kroyn, dertseylungen [The Crown: Stories]. Tel Aviv: Yisroel-bukh, 1973.

Shtern laykhtn in thom, gezamlte dertseylungen, 1940–1944 [Stars Lighting Up the Abyss: Collected Stories, 1940–1944], 2 vols. Tel Aviv: Yisroel-bukh, 1976.

Tsvishn tof un alef, gezamlte lider [Between Z and A: Collected Poems]. Tel Aviv: Yisroel-bukh, 1978.

Avrom Sutskevers lider fun togbukh, esey [Avrom Sutzkever's Poetry from His Diary: An Essay]. Tel Aviv: Biblos, 1979.

Himlen nokhn shturem, noveln, eseyen, lider [Heavens after the Storm: Stories, Essays, Poems]. Tel Aviv: World Council for Yiddish, 1984.